The Atomic Bal

by

I.O. Adler

Old Chrome Book Two

CW00523941

Copyright © 2022 I.O. Adler

All rights reserved. No part of this publication may be reproduced, stored in a retrieval system, copied in any form or by any means, electronic, mechanical, photocopying, or recording, or otherwise transmitted without written permission from the publisher. You must not circulate this book in any format.

Published by Lucas Ross Publishing.

Edited by Dave Pasquantonio, www.davepasquantonio.com[1]

Author website: ioadler.com

This is a work of fiction. Names, characters, places, brands, media, and incidents are either the product of the author's imagination or are used fictitiously. Any resemblance to similarly named places or to persons living or deceased is unintentional.

---

1. http://www.davepasquantonio.com

Chapter One

Miles Kim took a polite sip of the bitter oolong tea from the demitasse, his metal fingers carefully gripping the fishbone-thin handle of the cup. He sat on the edge of the butterscotch loveseat, not wanting to lean further back to disturb the nest of embroidered pillows or allow his dusty pants to further soil the velvet.

The woman seated on the winged sofa across from him was Beatrix Fish, a fellow Seraph Express passenger and survivor of the bandit and robot attack which had almost cost them their lives.

Her creased face was grave with concern. She ignored her own teacup, which had been placed before her by the well-manicured maid wearing an apron. Not to be confused with the maid in the long tunic who had greeted Miles at the front door. Both servants had discreetly departed the lounge. Or was it a sitting room? Miles had never been inside a house quite like the Fish mansion.

"Thank you for coming, Mr. Kim," Beatrix said. "It's my daughter. She's missing. And I thought a person like you..."

"You can say cyborg. It's not a bad word. At least not with everyone."

"A person who is a former police officer with Meridian's armed services. After our recent misfortunes, I see I can count on you."

"Seraph has its own law enforcement," Miles said.

Beatrix waved the comment aside. "The militias can't be trusted. And the marshal service will cry about jurisdictional issues. What fop. Plus, they're incompetent when it comes to dealing with a matter with discretion."

"A kidnapping isn't something to drag your feet on, Mrs. Fish. I worked with Marshal Barma when we pursued the people who attacked our train. He may be a stick in the mud, but he's not incompetent."

"The good marshal may be able, but it's the rest of his office I don't trust. Rumors. Grift. They answer to the mayor's office and the sheriff. Not much better than the militia. I'd prefer to work with you."

Miles set the cup on the saucer. "If your daughter was taken, I don't get you shopping around. This is straightforward police work. I'm new in town, don't know the place, don't have resources. You've got the wrong man."

"It's for those reasons I have precisely the right one. This wasn't some smash and grab of a child, Mr. Kim. My Agatha was taken by my husband."

"Is Mr. Fish not around?"

"Not since our separation. He's taken up in our New Springs estate on the north side of Seraph."

Miles waited for more, but she was looking at him expectantly. "I don't know you or your husband. What are we even talking about here? Did he strong-arm his way into your home last night?"

"Nothing so brutish. He lured her away and had one of his...henchmen pick her up and bring her to him. He doesn't love her, won't care for her, he just wants her because she and our oldest daughter stayed with me after our separation."

"All the more reason to involve Seraph law. If I show up at his front door asking for Agatha, he calls the cops. The real ones, whoever they might be."

"But that's precisely what he won't do. He doesn't trust the militias or the marshals either. That's why he hires the best bodyguards. Allowing Seraph law into his business means an avalanche of itching palms to keep tongues from wagging."

Miles ran his left hand along the seam of the cushion. "So, he's into some shady dealings."

She let out a laugh. "You really aren't from here, are you? Shady dealings, indeed. He has a chokehold on machine imports from Meridian and is now actively cornering the market in New Pacific. Seraph lies in the middle. Every sale, every purchase means more credits in his coffer. But we're not here to discuss commerce. Can I count on you?"

"I'm one man."

"And you'll be rewarded." She mentioned an amount. "That's for agreeing to help. Twice that upon bringing Agatha home."

He picked up the cup and drained it. It was a lot of credits. Way more than what he would have received by selling his cybernetics. Enough to make his son Dillan comfortable for years.

"I'll think about it."

She scowled. "What do you mean?"

"It means I'll think about it. Agatha wasn't swiped by some Metal Head. It sounds like she'll be safe for a day or two. Let me get my bearings and call you this afternoon."

"This is pressing. My girl needs to be rescued."

"If it can't wait a few hours, then find someone else. If it can and I decide to help, then I'll get Agatha back. Those are the options. Is there a way to reach you?"

Beatrix leaned back and appeared winded. "Talk to Celia on the way out. She'll provide a contact number. And Mr. Kim? Don't make a mother beg. It's unbecoming."

Chapter Two

One of Beatrix Fish's maids waited at the front door to the mansion with a physical contact card ready. She had also offered to send Miles back to the center of town with Mrs. Fish's driver, who had picked him up at his hotel.

Miles declined. He wanted to walk. Time to think. Time to see more of Seraph to understand the town, which was a world of difference from Meridian.

Ten minutes into his walk and he was second guessing his choice. Sweat trickled down his face and back. The pre-noon sun weighed like a thick blanket. His hips ached with every step on the unyielding concrete and hard dirt roads.

The larger homes gave way to row after row of sealed greenhouses. A damp soil smell permeated the air. Electric trucks and wheeled or walking delivery drones roamed the alleyways. Workers loaded pallets with boxed goods. A radio from a nearby greenhouse played the yammer of a dramatic reading or religious program.

A refrigerator van rolled past, marked with a logo boasting a literal cornucopia of strawberries, honeydew, tomatoes, peppers, and cucumbers, the engine a high whine that drowned out the broadcast.

"Help!"

The cry carried from a narrow lane between a block of warehouses and a plastic-windowed farm where a large sliding door stood halfway open. Miles looked around. Saw no one. And then came a muffled scream, which cut off.

Miles ran. He ducked to get under the raised door and found himself in an overgrown greenhouse where bushy lettuce grew in rows on a raised bed. He heard splashing, so he climbed a metal ladder to get a better look. Below the troughs of lettuce was a pool of dark water, and someone was thrashing. Ripples grew, and a head of hair was the last thing Miles saw as the person sank.

He was about to dive in when he spotted a pole and hook. He grabbed it and lanced it downward. A hand grabbed the end, then Miles pulled, yanking a small man wearing baggy shorts and a tank top to the surface. The man sputtered, hacked, and was dead weight as Miles snagged him by the collar and hauled him to the edge of the pool. With a last heave, he got the man flopped over the side. Water sprayed every time the man coughed.

"I got you," Miles said. "You're okay."

The man nodded, then shook his head as he pulled himself from the water. His arms were trembling, and he needed help standing. But he was pushing at Miles, leading him towards the exit.

"Take it easy," Miles said. "Sit. Breathe."

"Can't," the man rasped. "They're coming."

Voices from the opposite end of the greenhouse shouted. A half-dozen men were hurrying towards them. Miles only had seconds to decide what to do. He shoved the man along with him as they passed beneath the door and raced out of the alley.

The long avenue and alleyways ran in every direction. Hardly a place to easily evade a group of determined pursuers. But the sopping wet man tugged on Miles and brought him to a parked three-wheel motor wagon with no doors. Miles joined the man in the cab. The man thumbed a control panel and started the engine, putting the vehicle into gear and racing forward as the gang of workers erupted onto the street.

They sped past the men to a chorus of jeers and shaking fists.

The man coughed again, spat, then laughed.

Miles hung onto the lip of the cab's roof as they took a corner. "What's so funny?"

"Didn't expect I'd almost drown in the middle of the desert."

"Was it worth it, trying to steal lettuce?"

"Lettuce? Blech. Can't stand the stuff. But the fish they keep in the pond below? That's good eating. Shame about my line and hook."

"You were stealing fish." It wasn't a question.

"A man's gotta eat. And they've got some fat tilapia swimming in those ponds. Thank you, by the way." The man glanced at Miles a few times before finally inspecting him more thoroughly. "Say, you're a—"

"A guy who was in the right place at the right time," Miles finished for him. "You'd better think twice about coming back and pilfering lunch from that farm."

"Yeah. I've got plenty of other spots, though. Seraph provides when you know where to look. Name's Tristan."

"Miles."

They took another corner. A stepladder, buckets of rags, hoses, and a compressor shifted about in the three-wheeler's bed. Tristan slowed down as he wended around a large container being unloaded.

"You're a painter?" Miles asked.

"Painting, sealing, patch work, even a little plumbing. No job too small."

"Then why don't you build your own fishpond so you don't have to steal them?"

Tristan flashed a mouthful of yellow teeth. "Where's the fun in that? Besides, then I'd be the one fending off the filching anglers. You don't appear like you work in the Green district, Miles."

"Passing through. Taking in the sights."

Tristan wiped his thin, wet hair from his eyes. Premature pattern hair loss, soft around the middle, with ink up and down both arms. Younger than Miles had first guessed, perhaps early thirties.

"Taking in the sights," Tristan said. "That's rich. But minding your own is good sense. There's a towel behind the seats. Wouldn't want you to rust. So, then, Mister Tourist, where can I drop you off?"

Chapter Three

Tristan pulled up to a corner. "Marshal's office is that white building there. That's as far as I get you."

Miles climbed out and gave a goodbye wave before straightening his hat. He still had the damp towel in his hand, but Tristan's three-wheeler was already pulling away.

Seraph Marshal Office, the plaque read. The tinted glass doors made it impossible to tell if the office was open. Miles pushed the door in and entered.

A black drone with an illuminated red eye sat atop a metal screen at the end of a short hallway. A heavy door with a view slot stood closed.

"Halt. Present identification," a canned woman's voice said.

Miles didn't have any. "I want to speak with Marshal Barma. Tell him it's Miles Kim."

"Identification."

He tried to assess if the drone perched atop the shelf was armed, but without a close inspection, it proved impossible. "I'm not carrying an ID. Tell the Marshal I was by."

When he turned to leave, the exit door was locked.

"Remain where you are. Hands at your sides."

Miles tugged and pushed at either door for good measure. Had word gotten out that he was alive and well in Seraph? Had Marshal Barma changed his mind about him and learned of the bounty on Miles' head?

The drone's light winked out. The heavy interior door buzzed and clicked open.

A stern woman in a white button-down shirt and a badge on her chest swung the door wide. She wore a compact burner in a holster high on her right hip. "Please come with me."

"Barma's in?"

"Yes, Mr. Kim. And he agrees to see you despite your lack of any identification. Are you armed?"

"Just my charming smile."

She scowled as she conducted him inside. The office appeared small, considering the size of the building, but beyond several desks and cubicles was an inside atrium with large ferns and a tulip-shaped fountain that trickled water.

Barma rose from a cubicle. A large man, he wore suspenders, and his shirt front dangled over his belt. But like the receptionist, he was also packing. A stubby hand cannon dangled from a shoulder holster.

"The robot lives," the marshal said. "And you made it past Glenda. Congratulations. I thought you'd be plugged in somewhere recharging your batteries."

"My hotel didn't have an adapter."

"What do you want?"

Miles rounded the cubicle. There was no guest chair. "You check on Hill?"

Hill was the young girl from the desert village whose father Zoon had ambushed Miles and the Marshal. Zoon had tried to hand them over to an insane man-machine overlord living in an abandoned mine. Zoon had then been gunned down by Dawn Moriti, the vanished Meridian agent who held a warrant for bringing the AWOL Miles Kim back to River City. But Dawn had let him go for what Miles guessed was the short-term gain of a valuable haul of mystery tech from the aftermath of the train robbery.

"I haven't checked again since early this morning. Been busy. And this is no longer your concern. If you have a police matter, go to the sheriff's office and he'll assign a militia rep. Even better, the nearest information kiosk will summon a militia patrol. There's one right outside."

Miles waited. The marshal sighed and continued.

"All right, she's fine. I had a chat with the psychologist at the home. Hill had a rough first few hours and then she was sleeping. He guesses she's never been anywhere but that stupid village, has never been around other adults or children, and she's going to have a battle on her hands acclimating. But she's young, so there's that. Resilience and all. So are we doing twice-a-day updates now? You could have just called. Because I really do have work."

"What do you know about the Fishes?"

The Marshal grunted. "I'm guessing you got in contact with Beatrix."

"I just wrapped up a visit with her at her home. Says her daughter Agatha is missing and was taken by her husband."

The marshal scowled before leading Miles to the atrium. He slid the door shut, then they sat at the curved stone benches around the fountain. The receptionist gave them a hard look through the glass before returning to her own work. Miles had spotted no one else in the office.

"So what do you want to know?" Barma asked.

"I didn't agree to the job and told her I'd get back to her."

"Huh. That's bold. I'm sure she offered you a pretty good payday."

"I want to know what I'm stepping into."

"Pretty wise for a robot. You're tip-toeing into something deep and nasty, if you go to work for her."

"And is that why she wouldn't go to any of the local law?"

"Partly," Barma said. "Anyone who's been around Seraph for long knows about Beatrix and Gennady Fish. They're the top of the heap as far as money goes. Old-school Seraph, before the town was a town. And they did things differently back then. Since she asked for you, I'm guessing the sheriff wouldn't touch this, and I doubt either of the militias would, either. Who'd want to wind up on the nasty side of either of them?"

"So, both Mr. and Mrs. Fish are rich and influential. But what about the kid?"

"Agatha? Younger of the daughters. Doubt either mother or father cares much about her, except they'd rather die than let the other parent have custody. Both girls are with the mother, from what I've heard. So Gennady made some kind of play. Bad news."

"How?" Miles asked.

"If a Fish decides to shake things up, the town feels the vibrations."

"Is that why we're taking this sidebar in your little grotto?"

Barma let out a humorless chuckle. "I trust Glenda with my life. But when the Fish name gets thrown around, all bets are off."

"And you couldn't have warned me about this when you told me she called your office looking for me?"

"I almost died down in that mine, Kim. I have a mountain of paperwork. The autodoc told me to take a month off and get counseling for what I've been through. I'm running on fumes. Give me a break. So what are you going to do?"

"What I used to tell the patrol officers under me when I was gainfully employed. No payday is worth dying for."

Chapter Four

Miles squinted as his eyes adjusted to the sunlight outside the Seraph marshal's office.

He started walking in the direction he hoped would take him back to his hotel. When the dark sedan cut him off at the mouth of the alley and two figures in tan suits and white ties emerged, he stepped back and instinctively placed a hand on his hip. But he wasn't carrying a burner.

The largest of the two, a bruiser with no neck and a white crew cut, caught Miles and thrust him against the wall of the alley. Before Miles could protest, the second stranger, a wiry female with a blonde ponytail, socked him in the gut hard enough that he would have doubled over if he hadn't been held.

Miles grabbed for the bruiser's wrist and clamped down with his metal hand. Even as he applied pressure, Ponytail jammed a shocker into his neck. Electricity clattered as pain erupted through his head and body. He fell helplessly forward. His two assailants stepped back and let him drop. Then the bruiser kicked him in the ribs.

"Stay away from Beatrix Fish, 'kay?" Ponytail said.

Miles fought to speak through a clenched jaw. "Who's asking?"

"Cyborg must have a hearing impediment," Crew Cut said as he wound up for another kick.

A bleating horn preceded a squeal of tires as Tristan's three-wheel cart skidded into the alley, smashing the sedan's open door.

Tristan slid out of the vehicle's cab. "Whoops, sorry about that. My foot slipped off the brake pedal. What're you doing blocking the alley—"

Ponytail met him at the rear bumper and gave him a shove. "Move that piece of junk."

"Sure, no problem. Let me just give you my insurance number."

A handful of pedestrians were watching from the sidewalk.

Tristan began sifting through the three-wheeler's glove box. "Got my device in here somewhere."

"Don't bother," Ponytail said as she went to the sedan's driver's side door. "Come on, Raz."

Raz gave Miles a parting kick before the two assailants climbed into their car, backed into the street, and sped away, broken door flapping on its busted hinges.

Miles forced himself to rise but couldn't get a better look at the departing vehicle as a whirl of dust rose into the air. He double blinked to clear the reboot interface from his Insight module. Needed to clear his head.

"What are you doing here, Tristan?"

Dimples formed as Tristan beamed. "Lucky I was lingering across the street. Was checking Seraph net for day jobs. What was that about?"

"None of your business. What you did was stupid."

"Maybe, maybe. Pretty bold smash and grab. Don't normally see bandits dressed so nicely."

"They worked for the Fishes."

Tristan frowned. "*The* Fishes?"

"Yeah. None other." Miles limped to the three-wheeler's passenger seat and sat gingerly down. "Now, why don't you give me a lift? I'll pay you for the ride."

"Where to?"

"Beatrix Fish's home. I have a job offer on the table, and I'm going to accept."

***

A sharp pain persisted in his ribs. It hurt just to inhale. Miles couldn't have worn the seatbelt even if there was one as Tristan puttered through light street traffic.

He called Beatrix Fish. Her virtual assistant answered. "Mrs. Fish is unavailable right now. You may leave a message."

"I'm coming over," Miles said. "I'll find Agatha. But I have more questions."

"She will consider your request. Goodbye."

Stupid machine. He winced as he put the phone away, then dabbed blood from his lower lip.

Tristan slowed down to a crawl. "While your offer of gainful employment is generous, I'm having second thoughts. You should have second thoughts, too."

"If you don't want the work, then you can leave once you drop me off. You weren't scared when you thought those thugs were robbers."

"I didn't know who they worked for. Pretty bold to jump someone right outside the marshal's office."

"Interesting, isn't it?"

"It's not the word I'd use."

They once again passed through the Green district, taking the main boulevard and avoiding the warehouses. Miles gave directions, as his Insight module was back up. He had seen enough of the neighborhood to get oriented instantly.

Soon they were driving among the large homes and lush landscaping of what Insight labeled the Woodbine neighborhood. Beatrix Fish's two-floor mansion peered over the elm trees. The shining steel gates stood open, and Tristan drove them up the roundabout and pulled up in front of the entrance. He kept the engine idling.

"Will you be here when I'm done?" Miles asked.

"I haven't decided yet. Will you be allowed to leave? Someone could get lost in a place like this."

Miles didn't answer as he climbed the steps to the door. It opened before he could touch the bell.

A young woman stood in the doorway. Her braided hair went down to her waist. She was wearing a blue kimono and had a vape stick between her fingers.

"I'm Miles Kim. Mrs. Fish should be expecting me."

She looked Miles over before stepping aside. "I know who you are. I'm Kitty. Beatrix is my mother. And you're the one she hired to find my sister Agatha."

"Is your mother around?" he said as he stepped inside.

Kitty closed the door behind him. "She's with her trainer at the pool. It'll be another thirty minutes."

Celia, the maid in the long tunic who had greeted Miles the first time he had come to the mansion, came hurrying from down the marbled hallway.

"It's okay, Celia," Kitty said. "I'll see to our guest until mother's ready. Mr. Kim, won't you join me? Or do you prefer Miles?"

"Miles is fine."

She led him to a sweeping stairway. The high walls were decorated with long abstracts of soft colors, which reminded Miles of what a flower garden would look like if someone was on hallucinogens and losing their vision. An arched skylight let in the sun that spilled down onto the artwork spectacularly.

The top of the stairs led to an upper hallway and an interior balcony, which looked out at the foyer. More of the art decorated the walls.

Kitty stopped at a door in the hall. "Coming?"

"Perhaps I should wait for your mother in the reception room."

"Suit yourself."

He lingered for a moment alone, staring at blotches of vermillion and copper. Downstairs, Celia's footsteps were audible as she walked away. Miles went from frame to frame, taking in each painting before arriving at the room where Kitty had vanished.

"In here."

Kitty sat at the foot of a canopy bed that was covered in a frilly pink and powder blue comforter and matching duvet. A dozen pillows and large stuffed bears, lions, and tigers leaned on each other in a precarious pile. Bookcases were crowded with figurines, dolls, and hardbound books with embossed spines. A red wood writing desk held art supplies.

Miles said, "I'll stay out here and wait for your mother, if you don't mind. And I'm guessing I'm older than your dad."

Kitty rolled her eyes. "I'm not as young as I look. This is Agatha's room. I thought you should see it, if you're going to be looking for her."

He stepped in and gave the room a quick once-over. The room smelled of roses, a perfume or heavily scented soap, perhaps. On the desk between cups holding pens and colored pencils stood a small audio device. He clicked it on.

"...soil was once sand," a raspy voice said from the speaker. "Sand was once rock, all things to dust and from the dust, with God's breath, life. And all life is precious, my brethren."

He switched it back off, then picked up the device and examined the tiny screen. Cheap, mass produced, and something that might be purchased from a vending machine. It displayed a radio frequency. Not many radio stations existed, at least not in Meridian.

"Agatha liked to listen to that while she drew," Kitty said. "Mom hated it."

He put the radio down and checked the walk-in closet, which was as large as the kitchen in his old River City apartment near the military base. Some twenty pairs of shoes, fifty-plus outfits organized on hangers, toy chests, and the comfy smell of freshly laundered clothes. Some of the figurines on the shelves appeared to be made of gold and set with precious stones, among them a large striped cat, a poodle, and a pair of matching horses with opalescent eyes.

The centerpiece on the middle bookshelf was a porcelain ballet dancer frozen in a pirouette with her alabaster arms raised above her.

"Dance," Kitty said.

The ballerina spun slowly. A tinny music box rendition of a vaguely familiar ballet played from a speaker within the figurine's base. Insight identified the piece. "*Swan Lake, composed by Peter Ilyich Tchaikovsky.*"

"My sister had quite the collection," Kitty said. "Our parents always got us the best."

"Looks like a lot of dusting to me. But that's what the help is for, right?"

Kitty smirked. "Naturally."

Outside the window was a view of the garden and pool. Beatrix Fish was doing laps while a muscular-looking man in short shorts and a stopwatch stood and watched. Celia came hurrying up and got Beatrix's attention when she finished a lap.

"Two minutes, fifty-five seconds," Kitty said.

Miles looked up at her. "Excuse me?"

"How long it took Celia to make it to my mother and tell her you're upstairs with me."

"You're either very good at counting or you have an implant."

"It appears you do, too." She tapped behind her right ear. "My weave tech can be taken out any time I want. I doubt that's the case with what you have in that metal head of yours."

"If I click my jaw, I can unlock my car. I'll be downstairs."

Chapter Five

The mansion's kitchen was larger than Miles' hotel room. Beatrix was in a terrycloth wrap, her wet hair tied back with a band. She was bringing fruit out of one of three steel refrigerators and setting them by the counter. Blueberries, figs, plantains, guava, and a few hybrids Miles didn't recognize.

"The tayberry is a cross between a raspberry and blackberry," Insight offered. *"It is grown—"* He double blinked to shut it up.

Beatrix began loading the fruit into a blender. "I'm glad you returned promptly. I was worried you might have been intimidated by my offer."

"Your offer's generous, not intimidating."

"Surely you know what I mean. My family has a reputation. Perhaps you took the time to do some research."

"I did. I learned you were very wealthy."

She sneered before pulsing the blender and turning the fruit into a purplish gray glop. "And what else did you find out?"

"Some people think you're dangerous and that you couldn't hire a local to do the job you're asking."

"This sounds like a negotiation for more funds. Done. Fifteen percent in addition upon returning Agatha safely."

"That's not why I bring it up. A couple of goons had a run at me. Told me to stay away from you."

"Goons?" she asked, as if unfamiliar with the term.

"A henchman used to intimidate or harm. The word goes back to the 15th century, according to my Insight module."

"My husband's people. He spies on this house. I'm a prisoner here. Describe them."

Miles did. Beatrix paused in her smoothie prep to take in the description of the two who had attacked him before filling a small glass and taking a sip. Made a face. She added a heap of grainy powder from a jar and stirred it in. Tasted it.

"Much better. Would you like one?"

"No. So these two employees of your husband have threatened you?"

"Nothing so vulgar. But they linger outside on the street, watching. There are more than Raz and Trish. He has others, but they're his senior ruffians.

They'll follow me around Seraph when I leave the house. They're the ones who took my girl."

"About that. They broke in?"

She tossed a hand. "They lured Agatha outside somehow. It was the middle of the night. No smashed windows or doors, but it might as well have been."

"Is there security footage?"

"Yes, of course. Celia will share the recordings."

Celia had been standing by at the far side of the kitchen, head bowed, hands clasped, and at the mention of her name, she stepped forward and nodded.

"In fact," Beatrix continued, "whatever resources you need are at your disposal. My driver?"

"I hired one to get back here. I'll include his services on my expense sheet."

"Of course."

"So besides you and Gennady living in separate homes, what's your relationship like?"

Beatrix had been stirring her smoothie, but now paused. "What does that have to do with this?"

"Seems central to this whole deal to me. Do you talk? Exchange messages via lawyer? Do you have your own people watching him? I thought it might be prudent to understand the lay of the land between you."

"If I had my own gang of mercenaries or *goons*, I would have my daughter back already and wouldn't need outside help. And Gennady and I don't communicate."

"Does he talk to Kitty?"

"Leave her out of this. I'd prefer if you don't speak with her, either."

"She might be relevant to what I'm doing," Miles said. "Was Kitty home when Agatha disappeared?"

"I suppose she was. The staff would know."

Something else to ask Celia. Miles would also need to learn who else was on the mansion's staff.

"Does Agatha ever step out on her own?"

"Certainly not. She doesn't leave without me or one of the servants. She isn't allowed." Beatrix tasted her concoction again. "I've ruined it." She set the full glass and pitcher into the sink. "Is that enough background for you, Mr. Kim?"

"It helps. I'll have a look at that footage now."

"Excellent. You have my contact number. Keep me informed. Now if you'll excuse me, I have an appointment for a treatment."

Chapter Six

"I took the liberty of queuing the footage for you, Mr. Kim," Celia said. She spoke with a clipped accent.

The flatscreen in the viewing room dominated the far wall. Miles had the remote in hand and watched the footage spool past from several angles. Timestamp showed early that morning, at 1:17 a.m. when things got interesting. All the camera perspectives were outside the mansion, with one angle from a speaker box in front of the gate. A sedan pulled up. In the poor light it was impossible to tell the color, but the design and model appeared identical to the one the two goons had driven. None of the passengers were visible. The vehicle was mostly out of the shot, with only a rear fender in view.

The rest of the mansion appeared quiet, with ground-level garden lights and those leading to the front door serving as illumination. Anyone visiting would be seen, but there were plenty of dead spots, shadows, and paths to the house that had insufficient coverage. All this without considering ways to trick a camera.

Miles began to fast forward and watched the minutes tick by. At 1:43 a.m. the sedan drove off.

Celia pointed at the screen. "If you play that back slowly, you see the cab light was on."

He rewound and replayed the last minute in slow motion. As Celia had pointed out, the light inside the car had lit up, but the interior was a blur as the vehicle sped past and only visible for a single frame. He paused, zoomed in, and caught a reasonably good view of one of Gennady Fish's thugs, Trish, the woman with the ponytail, with another adult in the front passenger seat. And there in the back was someone shorter with long hair, but the face wouldn't get any clearer.

"That's Agatha," Celia said.

Miles replayed it a few more times, both slow and normal speed, freeze framing the one scene over and over. But even with a keen eye, the bad resolution couldn't be fixed with the current interface.

Kitty entered the screening room and slurped loudly at a straw in a cup. "Did I miss the action? Apologies. My mother posted her swim lap times and

I wanted to see if her performance was improving. Spoiler alert: no gains this week. By the by, that's a fuzzy picture. Here, let me see that."

She set her cup down and took the remote from Miles' hands. Blinked. The screen image sharpened until not only were the two goons' faces in perfect focus, but so was the girl in the back seat. Young, maybe twelve years old, but only half her face was visible, as it appeared she was trying to adjust herself on the seat while wearing a large backpack.

Celia silently picked up the cup and placed it on a doily.

Kitty handed the remote back. "There's your proof of my sister's escape from Valhalla in search of El Dorado. Will she find her fortune? Will she ever be seen from again?"

"Do you like your sister?" Miles asked.

"Depends on the day, week, or month. I'm more interested in what *you're* going to do next. Off to storm daddy's castle to rescue her?"

"Do you believe she needs rescuing?"

"My mother does. And you're being paid to. So what's the attack plan?"

"Tell me about your father."

She made a face. Sat on one of the oversized leather chairs and spread her arms along the back as she crossed her legs. "He works a lot. That about sums him up. Except when it comes to Mother. They have this *thing*."

"What kind of thing?"

Her grin widened. Her eyes darted towards Celia, who gave a deferential nod before ducking out of the viewing room. Miles recognized Kitty's expression. Had seen it on the faces of the younger soldiers under his command. She wanted to dish.

Miles took the chair beside hers. "Explain this thing of theirs."

"Oh, I'd hate to spoil the surprise. You're an ex-military cop, aren't you? At least that's about all I can find out. Your record appears to be redacted or missing. Did you have people like us back in River City, when Seraph wasn't anything more than a trading post?"

"I'm not that old. But yes, River City has families like yours. Wealthy, influential."

"Those are polite words. Spoken like an employee trying hard not to rock the boat. Or kill the goose that lays the platinum omelets."

"I'm going to get your sister back. That's why I'm here. I just need to under-stand why she was taken."

Kitty nodded at the frozen image. "Hardly a kidnapping."

"Does your mother have legal custody?"

"If you know Seraph, you understand that's a tricky question. But yes, she does. At least on paper. And the paper says Gennady Fish doesn't get to see his daughter."

"Is he a bad father?"

Kitty rubbed the lapel of her kimono. "Real silk. The fruit in that smooth-ie? Probably cost a day's wage for anyone working the greenhouses. A hundred-thousand-gallon pool out back, but you saw that already. It loses a half centime-ter a day out here in the desert. We've got hard data lines to not only the Seraph net, but Meridian and Pac City. For my birthday last year, Daddy got me this sapphire pendant."

She loosened the robe to produce a necklace set with a blue stone the size of Miles' thumbnail. In good light, he guessed it would sparkle and be pretty.

"Doesn't make him a good parent," Miles said.

"Doesn't make him a bad one."

"Would he hurt Agatha?"

Kitty tucked the pendant away. "Not physically. But what wouldn't he do to tweak my mother, all while making sure her every need is met?"

"This place is his?"

"Oh no, it's hers all right. She owns it and half of what he once owned, fair and square. He let her take it. It's only after the virtual documents were signed that things got interesting between them."

"When's the last time you saw him?"

She blinked hard. "Two months ago, for brunch. We met at the Caliper Club, just the two of us."

He caught the faint illumination across her eyes. More than weave tech, he realized. Coronal implants, and good ones. "Is that where he'd take you and Agatha?"

"Sometimes, but never both of us at the same time. And while I can put up with his stuffy little lodge, Agatha hated it. Always whining about the waste and lavishness. My father didn't know what to do with her when she started to lecture him. I'm sure he's getting an earful now."

"So why take her if they don't get along?" Miles asked.

"Because Daddy Dearest never gives up on anything."

Chapter Seven

"Anything, not anyone," Miles murmured.

Tristan drove them out the open gate, which promptly closed just as the three-wheeler's rear bumper cleared the entry. He stopped abruptly. "You say something?"

"The older Fish girl said her father didn't give up on anything when speaking about Agatha."

"Figure of speech, you suppose?"

"Not sure. Kitty Fish appears to enjoy her words."

Tristan scowled as he looked both ways, as if deciding whether to pull out. There was no traffic. "How 'bout supposing you tell me where I can drop you off? I think I'm allergic to this neighborhood. The more I think about it, the more I'm certain this is a mistake."

"Too late. You're on the payroll for our little affair."

"You told her about me?"

Miles pointed to the side of the gate. "There's cameras. Beatrix Fish knows what you look like. But I'm guessing Tristan isn't your real name, so if she wants to learn more, she'll have to track your vehicle."

"Why would you tell me that? That's not a comfort. I don't like this. I'm taking you back to the marshal's office."

"Take a left."

Tristan glared at him before pulling out. "I know which way to go."

"We're not going to the marshal's office. You're taking me to Gennady Fish's home. New Springs Estate. Leave me there, then you can go."

Tristan tapped the steering wheel nervously as the little engine fought to accelerate. "And you'll pay me?"

"A little now, more later. I haven't been paid yet myself. But I need someone who knows their way around town. Should be worth your while. New Springs is somewhere to the north."

"I know where it is," Tristan said irritably.

"And I don't."

Insight nagged him with a map of Seraph, but Miles didn't share the fact.

Tristan's eyes darted to the rearview mirror. Something a responsible driver would do. But with the light traffic on the surface streets, it at first felt like a mannerism, but then it grew annoying.

"Either tell me we're being followed, or cut it out," Miles said evenly. "You're spending more time with your eyes behind us than paying attention to where we're going."

"It's hard to tell. There was a sedan there like the one your two friends drove. Then there was a short-bed lorry. And now there's a robot delivery dog. What if Mr. Fish has a whole team after us?"

"Then we won't lose them. So how about not getting into an accident before we get to New Springs?"

Tristan nodded. Was about to say something but blew a long sigh. When his eyes wandered back to the mirror, Miles ignored him.

***

"There's a house in there somewhere, I suppose," Tristan said.

He had parked beneath the shade of an oak tree that towered over a decorative wall. Across the street was Gennady Fish's home: a white stucco wall topped with red brick, with oleander growing tall behind it. A black lacquered wood swinging gate marked the driveway, and the tops of trees were visible beyond. But Tristan was right. Miles couldn't even see a rooftop beyond all the foliage.

Insight shared the realtor's listings for the neighborhood. While Casa Fish wasn't listed, the nearest neighbors who had put their homes for sale owned sprawling single-level homes. Nothing in his price range.

After about five minutes of waiting, Tristan checked the mirror. "So we just sit here?"

"That's exactly what we do. Settle in."

"But someone will see us. They'll call the cops."

"When that happens, I'll deal with it."

A steady stream of robot delivery dogs came and went. None dropped anything off at the Fish home. Other traffic zipped past. Miles guessed it was the locals who drove the fastest, usually in higher-end electric coupes, but a few trotted past on horseback. Miles and Tristan rarely got more than a parting glance from anyone.

Service vehicles comprised much of the traffic—gardeners, contractors, maintenance vans, and an open bed truck delivering six geese. The geese went to the home with the decorative wall. Through the gaps, a spraying water feature splashed across a pond covered in water lilies.

"All we have to do to fit in is pretend we're goose wranglers," Miles said.

When a brown six-wheeled tank with yellow militia insignias rolled past, Tristan stiffened and shrank in his seat. The armored vehicle had a turret, but it wasn't manned. The militia personnel inside the vehicle were obscured by the heavy window tinting. Tristan's breathing came hard and heavy.

Miles kept his eyes forward. "Breathe in through your nose, out through your mouth. Blocking one nostril will help."

"They're going to...They're going to..."

"They're not going to do anything. They're just on patrol. They do that, don't they? No one called us in." Miles kept an eye on the rearview mirror. The tank was half a block down and turned on the first side street. "All right. Let's roll."

"You said they're not going to do anything."

"I'm sure they have a camera on their vehicle. And if we're here on their return trip, they might take notice. Drive up to Mr. Fish's gate."

Tristan didn't argue as he made a U-turn and pulled up to a freestanding call box. A silver lens stared at them. Miles reached across Tristan and touched the call button.

A dog began barking inside the house loud enough to hear. A large animal, Miles judged.

"How may I help you?" Insight identified the aloof feminine voice from the box as a virtual assistant.

The dog inside wasn't letting up.

"I'm Miles Kim. I was hired by Beatrix Fish to inquire about the location of Agatha. Is Mr. Fish in?"

"Please scan your contact information."

Miles held out his device he had purchased when he had arrived in Seraph. It wouldn't provide anything but a callback number.

"Thank you," the assistant said. "Your visit has been noted and forwarded to my client. Goodbye."

Miles put his phone away and studied the call box and gate. "Goodbye yourself. All right, let's go."

Tristan backed up and got them driving. "That's the plan? Just give them your number?"

"I see no reason to overcomplicate it. Everyone has told me what Mr. Fish is like. Time to find out for myself. If he calls, we might learn he's reasonable and it's been a miscommunication with his ex, and Agatha is home before teatime."

Tristan shook his head slowly, then muttered, "What planet are you from?"

Chapter Eight

The sun was set to broil as the early afternoon saw the most road congestion Miles had yet seen in Seraph. In River City, a pedestrian waltzing into the road against a red light risked dismemberment. Here, an unorchestrated chaos appeared to be the norm as men, women, and children leapfrogged and scampered across the street with little in the way of traffic signals. Delivery dogs, trucks, and desert runners crossed into the incoming lanes to avoid them.

"Is it always like this?" Miles asked.

Tristan chuckled. "Monday through Saturday. And on Sunday, it gets real crazy."

No traffic signs. Few markers for where folks were supposed to cross. And no zones dedicated to foot traffic. Yet by some unspoken agreement, instinct, or hive mind, it appeared to work.

Miles directed Tristan to a parking spot. "Hungry?"

Tristan jerked the three-wheeler to a stop and set the brake. "Always."

Miles pulled off his jacket and felt the sweat under his arms. A few of the downtown buildings were higher than two stories, and some had underground parking, no doubt with climate control. The nicer, sealed pedestrian vehicles rolled down the ramps, and the passengers never had to expose themselves to the heat or the perils of crossing the street.

On a corner, a pair of bedraggled women had a pushcart loaded with clothes, containers, and blankets. One sat at the curb and held a white plastic sheet which read "Credit for Food? God Bless."

Past the panhandlers, a fancifully carved sign above a bed of succulents read "The Caliper Club." The words were bracketed with a subtle gray set of calipers, as if the letters themselves were being measured.

Tristan stopped in his tracks. "Here?"

"My treat." Miles didn't wait as he hiked the steps to the club's entrance.

The chilly interior air hit him like a damp sponge across his face. A wall fountain gurgled pleasantly. Ferns grew everywhere. Slate gray stone reflected the cool white light filtering through the windows. A slab of polished black rock served as a reception desk, and beyond lay a spacious dining room crowded with patrons.

A thin man in a lavender ruffled shirt nodded farewell to a departing finely dressed group, who ignored him. The maître d's smile tightened when Miles approached. Tristan kept close.

"Table for two," Miles said.

The maître d' regarded them coolly. "This is a members-only club."

"And we're guests of Gennady Fish."

"Indeed? Mr. Fish isn't here. I'd be happy to take your name. You can wait in the lobby until he arrives."

Miles peered inside the dining room and saw what he was looking for. "We'll be at the bar."

"Sir? Sir, wait. It would be best if you—sir?"

They endured a few sidelong glances, but the handful of bar patrons mostly ignored them as Miles made his way to the bartender. The maître d' hadn't followed them.

The bartender had his long brown hair up in a bun. His tuxedo shirt was rolled up at his elbows. "Drink menu?"

"Green tea," Miles said. "Hot. And whatever my friend's having."

"Beer," Tristan said. "And...a mushroom sandwich if you're serving food."

"Right away."

The bartender went to enter the order into a tablet and went to work on the drinks.

"We're going to get thrown out," Tristan whispered.

"Then why did you order a sandwich?"

"It was the first thing listed on the specials board."

The tea and the beer arrived at the same time as a thick-necked club staffer who was stretching the limits of his fancy button-down shirt. His red eyeglasses were augmented-reality capable, and he wore a throat mic. He was what passed as the Caliper Club bouncer, Miles realized.

"I'm afraid the club is members only," he said to Miles and Tristan.

"And we're here to see a member who isn't here presently." Miles glanced at the security guard's name badge. "Is waiting at the bar not allowed, Mateo?"

"If you're guests of Mr. Fish, you'd have been prompted on the dress code when the reservation was made."

"Sorry, my implants are a bit rusty and in need of a service update. All right, we'll wait outside."

Mateo the security guard escorted them not only to the lobby but waved them towards the door. Tristan preceded them both in his haste to leave.

Miles caught the door. He paused to take off his hat and showed Mateo both sides of his face.

"What are you doing?" Mateo asked.

"Making sure you get a good view for your records. I'm sure once this gets cleared up, I'll have my membership details on file. So how's the grub here, anyway?"

Mateo rocked a hand from side to side. "Middling. I stick to the grilled cheese."

"You're lying. But I'll have to take your word for it. For now."

***

"That was...embarrassing," Tristan said as they took refuge inside a corner coffee and sandwich joint. He appeared to be breathing too fast as he watched the people in line and the street outside with equal levels of anxiety.

"Relax. I doubt they called anyone. We left when asked. But they got a good view of us."

"And that's a good thing?"

"Someone in Gennady Fish's circle will get the message. Just showing up at his front door is easily ignored. Someone actively poking around gets attention."

"Not the good kind."

The counter person brought out a pair of sweet pepper and soy burgers along with two cups of tea. Miles ate. When he saw Tristan wasn't touching his, he asked, "Not hungry?"

"I lost my appetite."

"You gave me my ride. Go, if you have to. I'll give you your credits."

Tristan lifted the top piece of roll and examined the sandwich. "Maybe a couple of bites."

They finished eating, then sipped tea and watched the late lunch crowd dwindle. Outside, the passersby were a mix of casual and business and everything in between. Those inside the Caliper Club had been the best dressed Miles had seen. And there weren't many of them coming and going on foot.

He checked Gennady Fish on the Seraph net and found surprisingly little except for a few mentions on the news sites, usually his name in association with a business called Founder Corp. They were the money behind several land development and manufacturing and construction projects, but never the front-line producer of anything tangible. He copied and pasted the Founder Corp address into his virtual clipboard.

A few social blogs tagged both Gennady and Beatrix, but the mentions were few and far between, with the occasional appearance of either at a public or civic event. One comment mentioned their marriage had ended twenty years ago. Which meant Agatha came along after the separation.

When Miles again became fully aware of the coffee shop, Tristan was watching him.

"You're still here," Miles said.

"You haven't paid me yet."

"I have the address of Mr. Fish's place of business. Let's drive by there."

When Miles told Tristan the street and number, Tristan let out a sigh and pointed at the tallest building in the downtown skyline. It was only a block away.

"But you're not really thinking about going there, right? You believe he kidnapped his daughter and brought her to work?"

"Probably not. But until I see for myself, I can't say for certain."

Miles' phone pulsed. When he answered, Gennady Fish's virtual assistant spoke. "Good afternoon, Miles Kim. Mr. Fish has agreed to see you. I will send the meeting information upon your acceptance."

He glanced at the waiting prompt and didn't hesitate to tap "Yes."

Chapter Nine

While it was hardly a skyscraper, the headquarters for Founder Corp occupied a twelve-story tower, which stood six floors higher than its neighbors. All glass and steel, with a high spire. Miles couldn't imagine any business in Seraph needing a place so large. It was as if the building was daring the Caretakers above to smite them.

"Go get your car and meet me at the front," Miles said.

Tristan spat. "You're not going up there alone, are you?"

"Would you come if I invited you?"

"I'll get the car. If you're not out in thirty minutes, I'm leaving. I'm too old for this."

Miles walked. He still couldn't get a sense of the town. Settled by people fleeing Meridian, yet here it was becoming something similar, only with more chaos not concealed. Soon the population would demand traffic controls and better policing. It would be River City with a new wrapper. And here he was, in the thick of it. He hoped Dillan was finding the life he wanted and promised himself he would call his son.

Outside the building, a row of drivers with bright carts festooned with lights, ribbons, and trinkets whistled and called for riders to choose their for-hire taxi. A rainbow-stickered van was parked in front of a sleek blue limousine. A crew of workers was using a vacuum mounted in the van to clean out the limo interior, while a driver in a checkered suit stood nearby and tapped away at a device. Above it all blared a radio program from inside the limo.

"...but that is how it will always be. The faithful will care for the faithless and poor. It is our burden, it is our blessing, it is our duty. For every unbeliever has a soul waiting to be awakened..."

Inside the Founder Corp building, Trish was waiting for him by the bank of elevators. She had her tan jacket buttoned, sunglasses on, her ponytail neatly arranged.

"Mr. Fish is waiting." She touched the elevator pad, and a door opened for them. She waited for Miles to enter first before accompanying him and pressing the button for the top floor. The door slid shut. It was hard to tell they were moving.

"Gig pay well?" Miles asked her.

She ignored him for a moment, then said, "What do you care?"

"Private security in River City paid ten times what I made as an army cop, plus perks."

"But then you have to live in River City," Trish said. "So why didn't you take the job?"

"My wife always said I was afraid of change."

"Then you shouldn't have come to Seraph."

The elevator opened to a polished hallway with an intricate floor design. Miles couldn't tell if it was wood or stone. A glass block wall on the left was illuminated with red, blue, and purple lights from an invisible source. The other wall held a large window, revealing a spacious lounge suite on the opposite side with an expansive view of Seraph.

At the end of the hall stood a receptionist desk. A compact man in a dark suit waited in front of it. His hair was slicked back. He wore rings on several fingers and sported a bolo tie with a cluster of sparkling rubies set in the clasp.

"Miles Kim. I'm Gennady Fish. I have a few minutes. Won't you join me?"

The door to the lounge opened automatically as Gennady led them inside. A full bar occupied one side of the room, replete with liquor bottles and a variety of glassware. On one wall was a smaller counter with teacups and a complex-looking espresso machine. It puffed wisps of steam.

Raz, Gennady Fish's other goon, stood behind the counter and was working at a tray set with two cups.

Miles joined Gennady at a set of plush suede lounge chairs set before one of the wide windows. Trish took up a position behind Miles at the bar, while Raz brought over the tray and served them. Each teacup had a head of caramel foam and a leafy design of white cream drawn on top.

"I hope you like chai tea," Gennady said. "Raz makes the best lattes."

"He should consider becoming a barista."

"He's a man of many talents. I only hire the best. Now I only have a few minutes for this, so let's get started. You came to my home and left a message."

"I was hired by your ex-wife to find Agatha."

"You're the retired cop who brought the train passengers home safely. You must have made an impression on Beatrix for her to reach out to you."

"I suppose. I didn't get much of a chance to speak with her during the attack on the train."

Gennady made a vague gesture. "Actions speak for our abilities more than any resume. On that note, yours appears to have been erased. My people are the best at what they do, and Miles Kim exists only in a few archived records outside of Meridian's network."

Thanks to Dawn Moriti. While having his records wiped meant he might have fallen off Meridian's radar, the thought it had been done so easily without his consent made his guts churn.

"I exist," Miles said. "And you're a busy man. I'm sure Agatha getting whisked away by her father's employees was a miscommunication with her mother."

"Do you have children? It's never simple. Agatha and her mother had a spat. Usually they blow over, but my youngest was particularly agitated when she messaged me. So I brought her to my home so she could calm down. Tell Beatrix she's fine. She'll be home in a few days' time. All will be as it was."

"I'll need to see her."

Gennady sipped at the edges of his tea. "I'm afraid that's not possible. She's a fragile girl. And I'm not in the habit of letting strangers visit."

"I'm not that frightening. We could bring this matter to a rest."

"The answer's no. Agatha is in my care, and I'll not have her disturbed."

Miles set his cup aside untasted. "Then let her mother call her. A quick chat to smooth ruffled feathers is hardly going to hurt Agatha. It's her mother."

"You've met Beatrix. It's never simple, it's never easy, and it most certainly won't be peaceful."

"I'm a father, Mr. Fish. Children are more resilient than that."

"Perhaps yours are," Gennady said. "I'm sure a police officer has the time and luxury to raise his children so they can stand alone against the tests life presents."

"Helping a young girl run away in the middle of the night doesn't make you a good father."

"I never said that I was. That's all the time I have for you. Tell Beatrix what you need to. But letting her know Agatha is safe will be the best for all involved."

"Except Agatha."

The commanding view made the traffic below feel less intimidating, the vehicles the vital connective tissue stretching through the veins of a young city, the pedestrians her blood, and the glowing haze of the distant bright desert a skin of wilderness either held at bay or pressing in, take your pick.

Both Raz and Trish closed in on either side of Miles as he stood up. With a subtle nod from Gennady, they relaxed slightly.

Miles kept his smile fixed as he considered both goons. "One thing we haven't addressed, Mr. Fish."

"What's that?"

"Both of your employees here were keen on keeping me away from Beatrix after my first meeting with her."

"A mistake in my instructions. But I trust them. If their instincts told them you were a threat, I would believe them. They saw fit to send a warning. Were they mistaken, or are you a threat, Mr. Kim?"

Miles didn't wait for another round of verbal riposte and parry. He had learned what he needed. And he knew that Gennady Fish wasn't going to let Agatha go without a fight.

Chapter Ten

Miles remained tense until he was walking out of the lobby of the Founder Corp building.

He had expected Gennady Fish's muscle to join him in the elevator for some competitive scowling, or to jump him as he stepped out of the lift and take him to the basement garage for another beatdown. But they were letting him leave.

Tristan stood leaning on his three-wheeler and holding a piece of cardboard as shade against the sun. "I didn't think you'd come out. Time's almost up with seconds to spare."

Miles hadn't set Insight's stopwatch. "Most of that was spent riding up and down the elevator. The buttons stick."

"We're done here?"

Before Miles could answer, the roar of a big engine caught his attention. One of the six-wheel militia tanks swerved from the traffic lane and rolled to a stop with half its wheels on the curb. A trooper wearing a yellow helmet sat in the turret. Four cops in identical plastic armor, helmets, and sidearms deployed and surrounded them.

One of them had an officer's pip on their helmet. "Miles Kim? You're to come with us."

"Am I being charged with something?"

"Not yet."

The officer nodded, and the other cops secured Miles and placed cuffs on his wrists. Miles kept quiet. He knew the drill but had always been on the other side of the exchange. Tristan stood stunned as Miles was hauled to the tank and shoved into the back. The rear compartment was a hard plastic sitting area with nothing to grab hold of as the vehicle lurched into gear.

He tried his best to keep from bouncing out of the seat and had Insight track their distance and every turn. The cops' voices carried. From their chatter he learned the officer's name. Lieutenant Chati.

They weren't leaving town. At least it wouldn't mean a lonely end in a desert grave. But he felt his heart sink when he saw the militia headquarter compound through the narrow slat window. It looked like a smaller version of Meridian's main prison.

The white concrete keep had high walls and antenna arrays, cameras, and shielded towers no doubt manned. A gate closed behind the tank like the steel jaws of a prehistoric shark.

Insight provided some light reading on Seraph due process, but Miles shut the embarrassingly scant feed down when he learned the most recent update was from twenty years ago.

The cops who assisted him down the step from the tank's holding compartment were relatively gentle. Lieutenant Chati led the procession. They ushered him to a side building, a plain single-level concrete bunker with steel shutters over the windows.

Miles was expecting a cell or interrogation cubicle. But he was plopped down at an unremarkable desk in an open office opposite a female cop. She wore a yellow uniform with captain's bars on her collar and a monocle on her right eye. Her short dark hair was shot through with gray, and she had a face of freckles.

The captain was typing with two fingers at an old terminal. "Free him, Lieutenant."

Lieutenant Chati cleared his throat. "Sir, this interview shouldn't take long. In fact, we have the cell ready."

"Don't make me ask twice, Chati. And then you're dismissed."

Lieutenant Chati motioned to one of the cops, who undid Miles' handcuffs. The rest of the militia troopers departed, leaving Miles and the captain alone.

"Be with you in a minute."

Miles rubbed his wrists and looked about the office. No visible surveillance. But even if he could make it out the door, he was certain it would be guarded. He took a breath to steel his nerves and eased back and waited.

The captain stopped typing, pivoted, and opened a file. Read for a moment. Then she removed the monocle and considered him with her black eyes. Miles met her gaze.

"I have the report from the events on the train," she said. "It appears Seraph should be grateful you were on hand."

"Just trying to get here in one piece, like everyone else."

"So modest. I'm Captain Santabutra Sin, Yellow Tigers militia. We keep order here in our town."

Miles kept quiet. Captain Sin appeared experienced enough to know the trick of letting the perp fill in the blanks and invariably trip themselves up with a clumsy lie or a confession to something.

"And you are supposedly Miles Kim. No identification. Name and face not on any of the current registries. No address, no vehicle, no nothing but a temporary device you purchased upon coming to town. Do you know why you're here, Mr. Kim?"

"Stunning good looks."

Not even the hint of a smile. "There was a complaint. It appears you entered a building downtown where you caused some trouble."

"No trouble. I was invited, so I wasn't trespassing. I had an interview with Gennady Fish. Is he the complainant?"

"No. Someone on his staff called and said you were making threats. We take this kind of accusation seriously."

Miles tapped his lips contemplatively. "Let me guess. Either Raz or Trish. They dress the same, so I get them confused. One makes a wicked latte, though. I made no threats. Mr. Fish and I had a conversation. And then I left."

"We'll be holding you until we finish our investigation, Kim."

"Is that the cell you have ready? Their word against mine? And how long will you hold me until I get to talk to a lawyer?"

She slipped the monocle into a vest pocket and began scribbling in a notebook. "Gennady Fish is an important man in Seraph," she said without looking up. "He's an important man to keep as a friend for the Yellow Tigers."

"A call from him, excuse me, one of his staff, means you scoop up whoever Mr. Fish tells you. Today it's me."

"My cousin Kamon served with a Miles Kim. A sergeant in a sister platoon who took over after all the officers were lying there in pieces or blast-mad from days of shelling during the final real battle of the Caretakers' War. Black Swamp. The last stand where the besieging Caretakers sent every remaining spider in their arsenal after the armistice had been signed. With all the technology, smart suits, helmet cams, and digital records, you'd think someone would have a picture. That was you, wasn't it?"

"If you're going to start believing what I tell you, how about the fact I didn't threaten or cause any trouble with Mr. Fish."

"Kamon didn't talk about the war unless she was good and drunk. And back when she was alive, I didn't care to listen. Stupid teenager. But one hot afternoon when I was laid out with a broken ankle, she was babysitting, plastered on sugar rum. Told me how the machines sounded when they crawled across the rotted trees and through the sandy marsh. What their red mechanical eyes looked like before they cut loose with burner fire. Said you'd have a half second to duck if you were lucky enough to catch the flash. Then they'd charge. The machines, she said, could slice a soldier through and pierce their armor like it was nothing but fish scales. Kamon began describing one of the soldier's screams when my mother came home and took her outside. I never heard another war story, and my mother never let that cousin babysit again."

"Kim's hardly a rare name in Meridian or New Pacific."

"Truly. But how many of them lost an arm and part of their face? It was the sergeant who was screaming as my cousin patched him up so he wouldn't bleed out. But he never quit fighting and kept what was left of two platoons from breaking until it was all over."

"Was your cousin the medic?"

"The doc was dead. She was a com specialist and grunt with a burner rifle."

Miles didn't trust his memory before his Insight module installation. Too many faces, alive and dead, blended into a blur.

"Where's Kamon now?"

The captain closed her notebook. "Died twenty years ago. My mother helped care for her after Kamon's father died. She thought Kamon had a peaceful last few years. But one evening just before midnight, she took her own life."

"I'm sorry."

"Filing a charge against you isn't optional. I can't just issue a warning when the call comes from Founder Corp. I have a lieutenant who wants my job bad, and our board of directors won't look kindly on a decision that might jeopardize our civil contract. What you were doing at their building is your business. But does it have anything to do with what happened on the train?"

"Indirectly. That's where I met Beatrix Fish."

Captain Sin cocked her head. "Beatrix? She's involved? I'm going to regret this, but why did you go to see Gennady?"

"He took their youngest daughter Agatha."

"And you thought you'd walk up to his office and get her back."

Miles wasn't sure if he was being mocked. "Sounded reasonable at the time. Beatrix hired me. That's the job."

"And how do you know it was Gennady?"

"Footage from a couple of nights ago shows Agatha getting into a car with two of his goons. Excuse me—staff."

The captain massaged her forehead with a thumb. "And you're going to bring her back. All right. Here's the deal. I have to hold you. We get to keep suspects for a week without filing charges. We can stretch that up to thirty days with enough fudging. But I'm not going to do that."

"You're letting me go?"

"Not exactly. I'm taking you to our booking desk and do some paperwork. It means you'll put down your name and a bioscan. And then you're going to plead guilty to all charges."

Chapter Eleven

Miles sat in the plastic-walled holding room. The space was cramped, dim, and reeked of damp bleach. The plastic bench was cracked and a cheery shade of lime green. Typical for a drunk tank. He guessed the militia company spent its credits on armored vehicles and weapons.

The plastic composite wall to the hallway was transparent but scratched and stained. On the opposite side of the clear barrier, a guard flirted with a prisoner in a neighboring cell. The man kept swinging a set of key cards around in his hand as he spoke, the clatter sounding like a deck of stiff playing cards being shuffled.

And the guard was supposed to cut Miles loose.

Miles had remained suspicious of Captain Sin when she escorted him across the yard between buildings to the large keep. There, under the eye of a sentinel drone armed with a charged stunner ready to fire, Miles confessed to a disorderly conduct infraction and allowed his thumb and good eye to be scanned.

"There's another place down the road from Frazier's," the guard outside the cell was saying. "Wine club. Good ramen, live music. Looks like you're out tomorrow morning. I could fiddle with the log entry and let you walk right now."

Miles got close to the door and drummed his metal fingers on the plastic. "My time's up," he called through the door. "Captain says to let me out."

"Keep your shirt on."

"Hate for you to get written up when all you have to do is swipe a card and get me through the front gate."

"I said just a minute. One more word and I thump you and put you in the infirmary."

Miles quit drumming. Paced.

A gaunt young woman in the neighboring cell shared a number. Her hands trembled. Her entire body shivered. Miles recognized a case of withdrawal shakes.

The guard punched the information in his device. "Maybe I'll get off shift and see you home. How's that sound?"

"Whatever you say," the woman said. "I'll get my stuff back? All of it? I really need my juice."

"We'll see. Let me take care of this first."

The guard buzzed Miles out. Miles walked quickly, but he wasn't fast enough for the guard. A baton smacked him across the small of the back just before they reached the door. Miles stumbled forward and landed hard on the concrete.

"Paid the captain off, didn't you?" the guard asked. "We had a special cell set up for you. Must have done something bad to someone. Don't think I didn't catch that you're walking out of here with nothing but a lingering fine, which will probably get written off."

"Then you'd also know that arresting me was a mistake—"

The guard kicked him. "Not what I wanted to hear. In a situation like this, it's customary to offer a gratuity."

"I'm a little light. Let me get your name and I'll make it up to you."

The next kick came harder. Then the guard yanked Miles to his feet, dragged him through the door, and brought him to the gate where he was unceremoniously conducted outside and left on the sidewalk. The guard tossed Miles' device on the ground before the gate shut.

Miles groaned. He had suffered worse. The beatdown from Gennady's goons compared favorably, yet even that hadn't been a top tier clobbering. But he had been much younger for his most serious trouncings. Tomorrow he'd be sore.

He stood on wobbly knees. The phone screen was scuffed, but the device worked. Tristan's number went to voicemail. Miles sent him a text, then started walking. Reddish brown clouds obscured the early evening sun. Dust stung his nostrils, and his skin felt itchy.

He estimated a thirty-minute walk to get back to his hotel room. Figured he needed a wash and a fresh approach.

"Mr. Kim?"

From across the street, Beatrix Fish's maid Celia stepped out of a four-wheeled runner. "Mr. Fish, can we speak?"

"Were you waiting here for me?"

"I talked to your driver. He told me the Yellow Tigers picked you up," she said in her terse voice. "They didn't log the arrest, so I came to make an inquiry in person."

"Beatrix sent you?"

"No, sir. Katherine did."

"Why would Kitty have you come here?"

"Because she wants to see her sister safe."

Were they talking about the same Kitty Fish? Miles waited for a passing car before crossing the street towards her. "And Mrs. Fish doesn't?"

Celia bit her bottom lip. "She did her duty as a mother and hired you."

"But wouldn't call the cops. So she did enough to balm her conscience, or is it so she can show on paper that she paid someone to find her lost kid? Or is there something else?"

"I...don't understand the question."

"It's all right. Neither do I. This is getting weird. Do you report to Kitty now that you see I'm out?"

"It is my duty."

Miles opened the passenger door and eased himself into the seat. "Does your duty include taking an old man back to his hotel?"

***

Celia stood in the center of the dingy room and appeared to not want to touch anything. Miles took a shower. The hotel's rationing system cut it off after two minutes, the weak spray barely enough to cut through the grime. He toweled off and got dressed.

"Your clothes are filthy," Celia said.

"I've been meaning to do some shopping. You're still here. Are you off for the evening?"

"I've been tasked to assist you. Your driver...he quit?"

"Made good on his threat. Your boss and her family have a reputation. And I guess the militia showing up was the last straw. I don't blame him."

Celia nodded. Her becalmed face looked troubled.

"It's just me and the four walls," Miles said. When she appeared confused, he added, "It's just you and me. No one's listening. You can speak freely."

"They are tortured souls. I feel sorry for them, the girls especially."

Miles realized he had no comb or brush. Did his best with his fingers. "Hmm. I'm sure there's lots of folks who would trade places."

"That is not what I mean. I know Mrs. Fish is very wealthy. Perhaps the wealthiest woman in Seraph. But every moment of her life is occupied with her struggle to justify herself to others, to her peers, her neighbors, the parents of other children in her circle. She is watched."

"Yeah. By her husband."

"Yes. Even though they have been separated for years, they still compete. It is in his eyes most of all she seeks legitimacy. Kitty and Agatha are caught in the middle."

"Kitty doesn't seem to be suffering."

"She is very sad. She is also very brilliant. She works for one of her father's companies. She designs technology and works long hours until she is exhausted."

"Works for her father but lives with her mother. Why not live on her own? Or stay with her father?"

"I would never ask her these questions. She says she despises them both."

"I'm guessing you keep that to yourself. Hates both her parents? Not a new story. But she sent you to help me save Agatha."

Celia nodded.

"Well, there's our answer. She loves her sister enough to stick around for her." Miles pulled on his hat and took a moment to check his reflection.

"You are injured. You should rest."

"Getting sleep isn't going to fix what's wrong with me. Besides, I still have some charge left in my battery."

Celia's face remained neutral.

"That's a joke," he added.

"I understand the humor. I just did not find it funny."

"It's okay, Celia, most people don't. I figure while I got you here, I might as well take advantage of it. What do you say we take a brief ride?"

Chapter Twelve

Celia parked at the side street a few homes down from Gennady Fish's place. The sun had set. The first stars and a crescent moon were visible above the clouds.

Miles stuck to the shadows, crossing the street and doing his best not to crunch through the weeds, which sprung up along the patches of dirt and landscaping in front of each home's fence. Going straight at Gennady Fish's house would be a mistake. There were cameras at the gate, and most likely some kind of security feature. Plus the dog he had heard barking.

But in Gennady Fish's case, he hoped this might be too much of a good thing. He crouched beneath an oak tree and watched and listened. From over Gennady's wall came a glow. Someone was home, or they left the lights on, perhaps on timers. Probably a single level structure. Miles wanted nothing more than to take a peek, but he couldn't risk being seen, at least not yet.

The decorative fence at the neighbor's home across from Gennady's was surprisingly sturdy. Miles hopped it. Heard the geese before he saw them. They grew louder as Miles approached, honking and hissing. If they were out and loose, he'd need a backup plan. But the neighbor kept his geese in a pen at night. They were making quite the racket by the time Miles got close enough to open the latched gate. The owner must either not have been home or was accustomed to the noise.

"I need a volunteer," Miles said.

When he reached in, one swiped at him. Another went for his face. Miles backed away as a third bird came low and hissed and snapped at his fingers. The gate slammed closed on its spring. All the geese were honking now. And still nothing from the house.

He knew he could try again, but the geese were too aggressive, and he didn't want to hurt them if he could help it.

As if in response to the clamor from the geese came the nearby irritable clucking of chickens. Miles discovered a wire coop around the side of the house with six white hens inside. Next to the coop were assorted gardening tools and a small carrying cage.

He'd handled chickens before, but it had been ages. At least these beasts wouldn't take a finger off.

"There, there, ladies. One of you gets to take a little trip. Now who's a good girl?"

Cage in hand, he entered the coop. Set the cage down. Two of the chickens came up to Miles' feet and stared up at him expectantly with their beady eyes.

"Aren't you both the most beautiful birds? Unfortunately, I can only take one of you."

He gently took hold of the closest one, and the bird didn't even squirm, only making a few inquisitive noises as Miles placed it in the cage. The others were scurrying about his feet. He eased himself through the door and latched it. Checked on his cargo. The chicken appeared wary.

"Play your cards right, and you'll get out of this fine."

The geese continued to screech as he climbed back over the fence. A few cars and an electric bike zipped past. He waited until they were out of sight before crossing the road. He climbed the wall to Gennady's house, opened the cage, and dumped the chicken out. It flapped as it landed before taking a few tentative steps past the oleander and onto an illuminated rock garden.

No alarms yet. But the dog inside the house wasn't barking either.

He heaved the carrying cage. It clattered among the rocks. When the dog began to woof and yip, Miles moved along the wall to the deeper shadows. As he had guessed, the house was single level and appeared to have two wings. A large place with many rooms, and there were lights on everywhere. If he got inside, he would need to be lucky. But first someone had to let the dog out.

Dogs, as it turned out. One little, one big, the first with an incessant pip-squeak yapping and the second with a snarl. The animals came bounding from around the front and charged into the rock garden. Someone had switched on brilliant lights along the outside of the home.

The chicken squawked as it bulleted away, bounding up into the thickest parts of the oleander with the two dogs dashing into the undergrowth. They bounced and snarled. Someone was shouting from the front of the house. A male voice. Gennady's.

"Fancy! Boomer!"

The dogs ignored the call. And both animals appeared completely distracted. Miles eased himself down and ran across a moss bed and leaped over a koi pond. He paused at a side door.

Moment of truth.

If the house alarm was off, he was in business. He kicked the door in. Felt a jab of pain. Both hips were still real, although the last doctor's visit threatened dual replacements.

The crash had been loud enough, but the dogs' commotion might have drowned it out. His breathing came heavy as he strained his ears for a chime or alert, which would precede an alarm. Nothing yet. No panel on the nearest walls, but that didn't mean the home wasn't wired.

He was in a short hallway. He came to a study with a dozen windows that looked out at the koi ponds and this side of the garden. The walls had framed paintings of pagodas and Japanese writing. The study was filled with heavy furniture and a suit of what appeared to be samurai armor. A collection of blades occupied a mantel and one wall.

He entered the main hall and checked room after room. Most were bedrooms, others were bathrooms, a cozy theater, and another office without the trappings of the first study. Here a single light illuminated a spartan desk with a ledger and a pair of tablet computers propped up with their screens displaying a spreadsheet and a letter or email in mid-composition. A mostly empty cup of tea with the bag on a saucer stood to one side.

Further down, two steps up led to a rotunda with a chandelier suspended beneath a domed, frosted skylight. The foyer and entry hall, no doubt.

The dogs grew quiet as Gennady continued to call for them. The front door stood open. The rotunda led to the second wing and a spacious living room and kitchen.

Gennady's bodyguard Trish stepped out of the shadows, a bowl of steaming noodles in hand. Her tie was loosened and top buttons of her shirt open. Her eyes narrowed when she saw Miles. She dropped the bowl. It shattered as she stormed towards him with a throaty roar.

Chapter Thirteen

Miles' close combat trainer had been a practical murder dwarf who specialized in low-g fighting.

"If you find yourself in a fistfight, pull a knife. If you're in a knife fight, pull a gun. If you don't have any of those, it's groin, throat, gut in that order. But don't leave home without a knife."

Miles didn't have a knife. As he warded off the first wave of sharp strikes, he realized Trish was not only trained but augmented. Each snap of a fist threatened to take his head off.

"Raz! In here!" she cried.

He had little room to back further away. Slapped a hand. Blocked a vicious jab, which sent crisp pain through his real arm. And Trish kept her defenses up. His butt touched a decorative half table. He grabbed whatever was on top of it, a crystal bowl in this case, and flung it. Trish deflected it. Miles took the chance to slip back towards the hallway. She grabbed his left arm. Twisted. It felt as if it was about to pop from its socket. She jammed him against a wall. She raised her other hand. Blades popped from the fingertips.

She was smiling.

Using his metal hand, he clamped on the fingers holding him and snapped them backward. She howled as he twisted and kneed her below the belt line. Slipped away just as she wildly slashed the air.

He gripped his tingling left arm as he stumbled down the second hall.

She'd be on him again in seconds. He needed to find a way out. But maybe he might lay eyes on Agatha.

Behind him, Trish again called out. "Raz! Get here now!"

From outside came hurried footsteps.

As he passed several rooms, Miles caught a whiff of rose. Paused. The cloying scent was the same as the one from Agatha's room at the mansion. He barged through the closest door and entered a bedroom. Large, overstuffed bed, plush horses, a pair of creepy but well-adorned porcelain dolls, a writing desk. A closet door stood open. Inside were a pair of small shoes, sparkly flats with bows, and a rack of pressed dresses, skirts, and blouses wrapped in plastic and all on hangers.

"Agatha? Agatha Fish? Are you here?" He checked inside the closet and behind the bed. "Your mother sent me to bring you home."

Footsteps in the hallway. Trish appeared, her hand with the busted fingers tucked against her chest. But by the look in her eyes, she wasn't done with Miles. She held her hand with the finger blades low, ready to strike.

He backed to a sliding door. The larger dog was still barking somewhere. He tried to imagine himself outrunning the thing. Wished his hips weren't aching.

She flexed her fingers. "Time to finish what we started."

"Patricia?" Gennady said from the hall.

"Get back, sir. It's not safe."

Miles grabbed one of the porcelain dolls. Prepared to throw it if Trish came any closer.

Gennady appeared behind her. "Go back to the kitchen."

Trish didn't budge. "Sir..."

"Now."

She gave Miles a final baleful stare before retracting her finger knives and departing down the hall. She and Raz began an urgent, muffled conversation. The dogs were with them and whining.

Gennady stepped into the room. His faint smile didn't match his hard eyes. "Quite the racket you've caused here tonight."

Miles wasn't putting the doll down.

"I assure you I'm not armed, Mr. Kim. No finger slashers. No cybernetically controlled lasers from the ceiling."

"Where's your daughter?"

Gennady Fish deflated and sat on the bed. "Gone."

"What do you mean 'gone?'"

"As in, I don't know where she went."

"You took her. And now she's missing?"

"I have the situation under control. The last thing I needed was for some washed-up cop my wife found on a train to complicate things."

"You and your ex did that fine on your own. Start from the beginning."

Gennady licked his lips. "Agatha left me a voicemail. Said she needed to leave home and wanted to come be with me. I had Trish and Raz pick her up."

"Why didn't you do it? Why did it have to be in the middle of the night?"

"Beatrix wouldn't have allowed it. Agatha said it was the perfect time. The servants were gone for the night or asleep. So they brought her here. She was always welcome to stay. But I was working an all-nighter. When I got home, she had slipped out. She won't return any messages."

"Signs of forced entry?"

"No. She made a show of going to bed. My guards retired for the night."

"Alarm and cameras?"

"She must have figured out how to turn the alarm off. And the only camera is the one by the gate. I'm not hiding in a fortress like Beatrix. I have Fancy and Boomer to make noise if someone breaks in."

Miles set the doll down. Wiped a film of dust from its face. "And your ex doesn't know, does she?"

"She can't. You can't tell her anything. I'm sure she's paying you, but I'll triple it. Find Agatha. Bring her here. Beatrix and I can figure it out from there."

"You know I have to tell her."

"You don't have to tell her anything."

"Look, you guys have got problems. But Beatrix needs to know about this. If Agatha's in the wind, then she needs to call the cops. Get more eyes looking for her."

"I've got people out searching."

"That's on you. But it sounds like you're trying to keep a lid on this. I can't tell if you're afraid of embarrassment or losing face with your wife. For Agatha's sake, Beatrix has to be told what's going on."

"I can't...I can't let you tell her. Mr. Kim? Come back here. We're not finished talking."

But Miles brushed past him. Trish and Raz were waiting in the rotunda. Both dogs were leashed and under a servant's control, but barely. Both began barking again.

Raz approached Miles, about to plant a hand on his chest while he reached into his coat. "Boss isn't done with you."

Miles punched him center chest and eased him to the ground, then yanked a burner from Raz's shoulder holster. He pointed it at Trish as he stood, but she raised her uninjured hand as if to surrender.

Gennady chased him out the front door. "Mr. Kim! Mr. Kim!"

Miles tucked the weapon in his belt and climbed the wall, dropping on the opposite side. Celia pulled up to a jerky stop, the electric engine revving. Miles climbed in.

"Go," he said.

It was time to let Beatrix know her daughter was truly missing.

Chapter Fourteen

A horse strode through Beatrix Fish's ballroom.

Miles couldn't help but stare at the spectacle as the ribbon and garland-decorated chestnut Arabian was led away by a pair of stable boys in maroon suits. A crowd of gowned women and men in tuxedos with coattails and tall hats applauded. Sitar music began. The partygoers filled the gap where the animal had been walking, and a buzz of frothy conversation echoed down the grand hallway.

A maid intercepted Miles. "You are not allowed in here, Mr. Kim. Mrs. Fish is not to be disturbed."

Celia took the maid by the elbow. "It's all right, Vinka. I assume responsibility."

Miles stepped past them to pause to take in the view at the ballroom's entrance.

Three candelabra burned in iridescent yellows and whites. The light reflected off the wine flutes carried upon trays by white-masked servants. Dancing ribbons twirled about as if gossamer caught on an unending breeze. Stars, moons, and suns with wavy halos slowly churned on the roof above. A musician in a golden sherwani sat on a stage between high glass doors and plucked at his long stringed instrument. The horse was being paraded near a banquet table set with platters of canapes, melon sculptures, a pig made of thin cuts of meat, and pastries of a dozen varieties.

And then one guest passed through the horse. It shimmered before the resolution returned. The ripples ran through the two stable boys as well.

Holograms.

All of this, or at least some of it, was a hologram. Miles bumped into a server. The server stumbled and caught the sole wine flute on his tray to keep it from spilling.

Miles helped steady him. "Sorry."

The server hurried off towards a set of doors where more of the staff were coming and going.

As Miles wandered forward, he noted most of the revelers had a sheen to them. Lights and shadows didn't catch the skin and hair just right. He reached out and put his hand through an older man carrying on an animated discussion with a huddle of eager listeners. The man didn't react and continued talking. Miles waved his hand back and forth. The image blurred away like the reflection in a pool before once again fixing itself in the air.

While the man didn't notice, one woman wearing strings of pearls and a peacock feather in her hair glared at Miles. Miles jabbed her with a forefinger. Felt soft skin.

The woman shrank back. "Ex-CUSE me!"

"Sorry, lady."

Miles moved past them. Spotted at least a half dozen "real" people freely mixing with the holograms. But the holograms talked, laughed, gestured. Real people, he guessed, but attending remotely. So where was Beatrix Fish?

Kitty Fish sat in a corner sitting area otherwise occupied by a group of much older women. One with a tall blue sparkling hairdo had Kitty by the arm, and they were whispering conspiratorially. The woman guffawed as her overfull wineglass sloshed. The spilled liquid shimmered and vanished. Kitty disengaged the woman's semi-transparent arm from hers, picked up her own wine flute from a side table, and downed its contents.

"Kitty, where's your mother?" Miles asked.

The women in the nearest chairs shot him dirty looks.

Kitty adjusted the strap to her dress and stood. The gown was stiff, and she fussed with the fitted bodice before making a show of squeezing past the others. Miles swept a hand through a fuchsia-haired dame and watched light play across his fingers. A group of younger men in coats and tails and tall hats with ribbons waited at the periphery of the group. While they too whispered among themselves, their attention was fixed on Kitty. She was the sun at the center of this gravity well.

"Excuse me, ladies, boys," Kitty said as she led Miles towards an unoccupied spot next to a window.

"What is all this?"

"One of my mother's regency balls. She decided last minute to host it virtually. It was meant to be Agatha's coming out party. Mother was going to give her that horse as a gift."

"Why would she throw the party after what's happened?"

"I thought you were supposed to be a detective."

He followed her gaze. Beatrix Fish stood at the opposite side of the ball-room on a dance floor where the light appeared brighter, as if the moon itself was descending through the crystal skylight above the candelabras. Next to her stood a young girl. She wore a dusty-rose-colored off-the-shoulder dress, and her hair was a tumble of thick curls.

"That's Agatha?" Miles asked.

"It's whoever my mom wants it to be."

Miles headed over.

"I wouldn't do that," Kitty called out.

But Miles ignored her. It had been too long of a day, and it was late. Agatha here? None of it made sense. He walked through a couple who were standing arm in arm and into a trio of young men. He bumped into one.

The well-muscled lad wore a thin beard beneath his jawline. Placed a palm on Miles' chest. "Hey, watch it!"

Miles shoved him. The dandy sprawled to the floor and into a woman who flashed in and out as the young man held up an arm as if to ward off an attack. But Miles kept marching. He had gotten the attention of most of the nearby crowd.

As he rounded the buffet table, Celia caught up with him and seized an elbow. "Mr. Kim, not like this. Please, I beg you."

He brushed her off. The sitar player stopped mid-melody. The glimmering ribbons vanished as Miles stepped onto the dance floor.

"What are you doing here?" Beatrix asked.

"I was looking for your daughter." But even as he got close to Agatha, he saw she was a figment of light and not really there. He passed a hand through her. The young girl had a pleasant, sleepy look and stared dreamily through him. "Where is she?"

Beatrix spoke in a low growl. "You're ruining everything."

"I just broke into your ex's house. She's gone. So where is she tying into your little ball from?"

Agatha winked out.

"Where's your daughter?" he pressed.

"How did you even get in here?"

Celia stepped up, her head bowed, and she dipped. "I brought him. He had news—"

"You brought him? You overstepped, Celia. Pack your things. You're dismissed from my service. As are you, Mr. Kim. I want you out of my house now."

"Not until you tell me where she is."

Beatrix Fish turned and stormed past the surrounding revelers, bumping into the same servant who Miles had nearly knocked down earlier.

Kitty Fish appeared at Miles' side and handed him a flute of wine. "And I thought tonight would be boring. Is this why you're no longer welcome in River City?"

"Your sister...she's logged into this party from somewhere."

"No, she isn't. She wasn't here. She was a simulation. And now you've let everyone know Agatha is gone."

Chapter Fifteen

Miles tossed and turned on the rickety metal framed bed in his hotel room.

At Kitty's urging, Miles had left to avoid having the Yellow Tiger militia called to remove him from the mansion by force. No matter how he begged, he didn't get his audience with Mrs. Fish. The ball had winked out as the attendees disconnected or headed out the front.

Beatrix Fish's driver had given him a ride to the hotel and wouldn't answer questions. Had there been scorn in the man's eyes? Definitely. Miles' actions had just cost Celia her job. Miles was out of work, too. And Agatha Fish remained missing.

But after dropping off into an exhausted sleep for a couple of hours, his brain woke him up. Too many questions lingered in a case that no longer involved him in any official capacity. But it was Beatrix Fish's reproachful look she had given him before leaving her own party that clung to him. Such rage, and all because she had been caught deceiving her friends and peers at her make-believe soiree.

A long-ago report from one of his officers came to mind. It still haunted him. There had been a minor disturbance complaint, a smell from an apartment on the base. The manager had finally called the cops when he discovered the door was jammed. A dead body, Miles would have guessed, and no doubt his responding patrol had likewise prepared themselves for what wasn't a rare event. But after they broke down the door, they found a young shabu-addled woman very much alive and living in filth. She had attacked them when they tried to check on her infant.

They found the baby cold and blue in its crib even as the mother fought to keep them away and shouting, "Don't wake her! Don't you dare wake her!"

Was Mrs. Fish suffering from a similar delusion? A darker thought weighed heavier: did she know something about Agatha's disappearance? Miles didn't know what to do with his suspicion. Didn't want to jump to any conclusions.

What were the facts of the case? Let the conclusions lie, skip the theories, follow the evidence.

Evidence. As if this was his case or his concern. Going back to the mansion wasn't possible. He'd be arrested. Captain Sin and the Yellow Tigers had shown themselves unable to help, hamstrung by whatever corruption ran through their organization. And going to Gennady Fish would get him killed.

A mourning father had once accused him and his fellow officers of being feckless after losing his soldier son to a repeat offender stoned driver who had smashed into a barracks.

Feckless. Insight reminded him of the definition. Sounded about right.

Miles had gotten good at tuning out the sounds of the hotel. Even at the early hour, footsteps clomped and doors banged and voices in loud conversations carried through the walls and outlets and up through the shower drainpipe.

But the footsteps that approached his door sounded extra heavy, and they belonged to more than one set of feet. *4:45 a.m.*, according to Insight. Nothing good happened at that hour.

He was up and out of his sheets when the door clicked and a pair of armored militia entered, weapons raised and aiming.

"Seraph Militia! Hands! Let me see your hands!"

Miles dropped to his knees and laced his hands together behind his head. A cop shoved him down and dropped a knee on his back. His wrists were zip tied. The other cop flipped on the lights and began rifling. Nightstand first, then bed, then Miles' clothes.

The cops probed and prodded him.

Miles grunted but kept his mouth shut. His ribs were too sore to endure another kicking.

"Get him up."

Captain Sin had her visor down, but he recognized her voice. Miles gritted his teeth as the two cops hoisted him upright and slammed him against the wall.

"How long have you been in your room?" she asked.

"12:43. Straight to bed like a good boy."

"There was dirt on his boots," a cop said.

"That's a crime in Seraph?"

It earned him a punch. Wasn't worth it.

"None of that, trooper." Captain Sin typed on a virtual keyboard. "Accessing lobby footage. You're telling the truth, Mr. Kim."

"What is this about? Crashing a party?"

"Among other things, yes. You've really shaken the tree, haven't you? Beatrix Fish says you trespassed and assaulted her guests and staff. You left her home before she could call us."

"And you're just now getting around to hauling me back in?"

"We received a call thirty minutes ago. Beatrix Fish claims you broke into her house after the last of the guests departed."

"And when Beatrix Fish calls, the Yellow Tigers send their commanding officer?"

Another punch. It took him a moment to recover. Still not worth it.

"Wait outside, Private Gowan." She waited for the trooper to leave. The other one kept a firm grip on Miles.

"You said it yourself," he gasped. "Front door camera. And me here in my shorts."

"Improbable, but not impossible."

"I was at her party. I bumped into a couple of people. But Agatha was there, or at least a hologram of her. When I tried to confront Beatrix, she fired me. I left."

Captain Sin raised her reflective face shield. Her voice softened. "You found Agatha?"

"It wasn't just a hologram. According to Kitty, it was a sim version of her sister. Beatrix is trying to make everyone think Agatha isn't gone. I couldn't even tell her what I found when I went to Gennady's house. Agatha's not there, either. Neither parent has her, but their heads are so far up their asses all they care about is not losing face."

Captain Sin stepped back and had a muffled conversation with someone over her com.

"I didn't break into Beatrix's house, Captain," Miles said. "Which begs the question, who did?"

She raised a finger for him to wait. He waited. "I have a squad searching the grounds. Apparently, the security system at the mansion was deactivated."

"I saw that system. It was state of the art."

"Some smart criminals in Seraph. A trained lawman with implants might make short work of an alarm."

"It wasn't me, captain. Timing of this is too coincidental. Your people any good?"

The cop next to him shifted. Miles tensed up in anticipation of a third blow. Instead, as if by an unseen command, the trooper let him go.

"My people miss little. But they also might not know what to look for. Put your pants on."

"Heading back to jail or the Fish estate? I need to know so I can dress accordingly."

Chapter Sixteen

Celia met them at the front door of the Fish Mansion.

Captain Sin had her two cops wait at their armored vehicle, which had parked next to a pair of desert runners marked with the Yellow Tiger militia insignia. To Miles, the smiling big cats on the doors appeared to be laughing rather than snarling.

Bright lights on every corner of the mansion flooded the garden and roundabout. Militia personnel tramped through a distant flowerbed. Dawn soon, but the sky remained dark and starless. On the drive over, Miles had seen the flashes of distant lightning.

"You are expected, Captain Sin," Celia said. She gave Miles a furtive glance as she conducted them inside.

Miles scanned the hall and upstairs balcony to see if anyone else was there. "I thought you got fired."

"Ms. Kitty intervened. My employer will undoubtedly weigh her option come morning. But Captain Sin, Mr. Kim isn't welcome in this home. Mrs. Fish was adamant."

The captain's tone was terse. "This isn't a social visit. I have a squad here responding to a break-in. Is Mrs. Fish available?"

"She was upset," Celia said. "Her daughter is with her in her bedroom. They had a very important social function this evening, which Mr. Kim spoiled."

"That's regrettable. You can let her know Kim is here under my supervision. I understand he was hired to investigate Agatha's disappearance. This wasn't reported to us or the Sheriff's office."

"My employer wished the matter to be handled with discretion."

"That's off the table now. And if I can't speak with Mrs. Fish directly, remind her I responded to her call personally. Tell me what happened."

Celia gathered herself before speaking. "Vinka, one of the maids, was finishing up cleaning, making a last check before turning in. The other guests and staff had departed by two this morning. I heard Vinka scream. She said someone ran past her down the stairs and out the front door. I took Vinka to the kitchen to calm her down. She is easily frightened. Perhaps a guest had fallen asleep in a bedroom, or a server had been hiding and trying to steal. It has happened in the past. But then I checked and saw the alarm had been turned off. I went upstairs to find Mrs. Fish had been awakened by the commotion. She was in Agatha's room. She says there were objects that had been stolen."

"Someone broke in and went to Agatha's room?" Miles asked.

Celia nodded.

"Show me."

***

Lights burned from beneath a door at the end of the upstairs hallway. The master bedroom, no doubt. Miles touched the light switch in Agatha's bedroom. Squinted and scanned the room. The canopy bed with its pillows and stuffed animals, the full closet, door ajar, with its shoe collection, the bookcases, and the desk.

Instantly, he saw what was different.

Several of the figurines were missing. Many had been precious metal, some set with gemstones, all finely crafted. The ballerina music box was gone too, as was the radio from the desk.

Miles examined a few of the remaining objects. Porcelain, ceramic, or made of cloth. "The thief took the most valuable ones, at least from what I can tell."

"You are correct," Celia said. "Besides the books, most of the items on that shelf were quite precious. A thief would see them and instantly recognize they were worth many credits."

"But why come up here to this particular room? There's valuables downstairs, from what I've seen. This place has trinkets and art objects everywhere. And surely Mrs. Fish has better things worth stealing."

"Don't guess why criminals do stupid things," Captain Sin said.

Miles touched each book spine. "I remain optimistic about the human condition. Some of these volumes are actual paper probably not made from pressed synthetic fibers. Why not take them too?"

The captain examined the window and checked it. Latched. "Limited time on the scene. Those didn't sparkle."

"Or they were smart enough to know these wouldn't be easily fenced. Still, I'm guessing these might be worth more than some of those figurines."

"You have updated black market pricing on your implant?"

"Just speaking from experience. But stupid criminals, right? Celia, you didn't lock the window after calling the cops, did you?"

"No, Mr. Kim. Mrs. Fish was in here, but she leaves such things as windows for us to care for."

"We'll need to ask her."

"But the thief ran out the front door," Celia said.

"That doesn't mean that's how they entered. We'll want to check every window and door. And then get a time on when the alarm was switched off. An inventory of the missing items would be helpful. Pictures even better. That is, of course, if the captain agrees."

Captain Sin peered inside the closet before stepping out into the hallway. "I'll get my people on it. And I'll be the one who talks to Beatrix. You need to wait outside."

Miles made a final examination of the young girl's belongings. Treasures, trinkets, knick-knacks. No one living in a habitat or on a ship would have ever seen such a collection of books. These had dust along the tops of the pages. A stack of colored paper waited to be drawn upon. Yet he didn't see any artwork. She didn't read, didn't draw. So what was Agatha interested in?

Because Miles was certain of one thing: the room held little that showed him who Agatha Fish really was.

Chapter Seventeen

Miles leaned on the front grill of the tank and watched the cops do their thing. Wander back and forth, mostly. Miles understood their need to look busy. Their captain was watching.

The militia troopers checked the windows and went over the grounds again, inch by inch, no doubt recording everything on their helmet and body cams.

The sun was rising. One maid brought him a cup of steaming hot green tea. He thanked her and watched her walk back inside. No doubt Beatrix and Kitty had their own twelve-course breakfast, which needed to be prepped. No rice with bean paste and kimchi here.

Captain Sin was at the front door and appeared to be composing a message on a virtual tablet projected above her arm. If the investigation had found anything, she hadn't shared it with Miles. And why would she?

He hadn't been able to offer much in the way of insights. Perhaps the timing of the burglary was a fluke and had nothing to do with Agatha. Miles didn't want to reach a conclusion. Agatha remained missing, and while the stolen items were valuable, there was no reason to believe recovering them would help with bringing the missing girl back home.

The thief could be anyone. The staff would have to be questioned, along with the guests. Someone had seen some easily fenced goods during the party. The suspect list would narrow down significantly, as the thief had to know how to disarm the alarm and cameras. Of course, if there was no footage, it meant the security system deactivation took place before the thief even entered the grounds. A timer? A bot secreted on the residence? An inside job?

Simple was better, and the last item most likely.

Full circle back to the staff having something to do with it. Celia appeared to have access to the security software. An even darker thought occurred to him. What if this was all Beatrix Fish indirectly stirring up attention in an attempt to get the militia on the trail of her daughter?

Too many things didn't fit with the theory. Too complicated. It still resulted in word getting out that Agatha was gone. And after seeing the lavish gala and the lengths Beatrix Fish would go through to keep up appearances, the sudden change in attitude didn't seem likely.

What about Kitty? She was a wild card. He still didn't have a read on her. She stated she wanted her sister back, but staging a burglary felt unnecessary if all she had to do was make an anonymous call to avoid upsetting her mother.

He took out his device.

His son, Dillan, picked up after two rings. "Dad? What's wrong?"

"Nothing. I just wanted to check in on you."

"It's seven in the morning. I'm racing around and about to head out for work. What's up?"

"I just...was thinking we should get together. Talk."

"Yeah, sure. But not right now. I'm glad you got set up with a place to stay. After what happened, you should be resting."

"I *am* resting. I was thinking about lunch or dinner."

Dillan hesitated. Soft muffled voices. He was talking to someone else. "Any of those sound good. But not today, and tomorrow's swamped. Look, Dad, I'm not trying to put you off. Can it wait until Saturday?"

"Of course it can. I don't want to let too much time go by. Also, I wanted to pick your brain. You said you're involved in a therapy program for children. You work with any doctors?"

"Yeah, of course. It's legit treatment through the hospital. Is this for you?"

"No. There was a young girl we found out in the desert. Her name's Hill. The marshal got her into a home. He said it's a good one, but I'm hoping for a second opinion."

"What are you getting involved in? You mentioned you were retired."

"I need you to send me a contact of a doctor, a therapist, or psychologist who knows children. Someone who's dealt with abuse. There might be more than one person I want them to visit."

More voices in the background on the line. A woman asking a question.

Dillan answered her, "Give me a second, babe. Dad, I really need to go. I'll forward you a name. But if the marshal is handling it, they don't need your help."

Miles said goodbye and ended the call. Only afterwards did he realize they hadn't firmed up plans for Saturday. Dillan would notice. Believe the call had only been to get a doctor referral. He let out a sharp exhale. It was the kind of distracted exchange which had killed their relationship after Seo Yeun had died. Correction: his work had poisoned their bond ever since his son had been born.

One of the militia cops gave Miles a longing look as Miles sipped the tea. It had grown lukewarm, but drinkable. Grassy, sweet, with no hint of bitterness. By the time he finished the cup, Captain Sin exited the mansion.

"Learn anything?" Miles asked.

"I don't think Beatrix Fish is going to be inviting you for breakfast."

"Was this an inside job?"

"Servants were accounted for," Captain Sin said. "Security system tracks them while they're on the premises. No one left before Vinka encountered the burglar, and everyone who was in the house was there when the system was brought back online."

"A guest, then, or an outside intruder."

"Or staff not on duty. Someone who knew where to find those figurines."

Miles pulled up his Insight feed. He had images of the stolen items from when he had seen them, but the resolution wasn't good. It was the kind of thing his implant would delete after 24 hours. He'd need to upload them soon.

A burglary was a wrinkle which didn't appear to have any relationship to Agatha's running away. But how could it not be connected? Had someone learned from Agatha the value of her collection and how to get into the mansion? Which meant Agatha might not be with the best company.

"Does this break-in bother you?" Miles asked.

"Besides having to respond to a call at the ass-crack of dawn? Yes, it bothers me. Every set of eyes wasting their time here could be looking for a runaway girl." The captain beckoned to one of her underlings. "Anyway, you're done here. Word gets back to Gennady Fish that you're out and about, I'll be angry. I'm going to have you brought back to your place. Lay low. This no longer concerns you. Word of advice? Find another hotel. That flea pit has seen its share of calls."

"I'm not easy pickings."

"If you say so, old man."

Chapter Eighteen

After freshening up and retrieving the burner he had taken from Raz, Miles went down to the front desk of the hotel.

A self-serve kiosk stood to one side where a guest might rent a room, get a key card, purchase vacuum-sealed disposable sheets, soap, hygiene products, prophylactics, lottery game cards, and sundries.

From behind the desk with the plastic screen, the foggy-eyed clerk glanced at Miles through a pair of yellow-tinted goggles.

"I need to know where to buy certain things," Miles asked.

He followed the clerk's gaze towards the looming vending machine.

"Things you wouldn't find in there, or at the drugstore on Gallina Road. Nice things. A gift, maybe, for a special friend, but at a good price."

"Downtown mall, I suppose."

"Yeah, been there. Not what I'm looking for. Maybe more like the kind of place where I could do some trading. See what unique gently used items might be for sale. A pawn shop, perhaps."

"No perhaps about it," the clerk said. "That's exactly what a pawn shop does."

Insight confirmed the assertion with a helpful definition.

"All right. Where's the nearest pawn shop? Maybe even one that's off the beaten path. Don't worry, I'm not a cop."

The clerk chuckled dryly and spat into a cup. "Didn't figure you for one. You're carrying a burner, though. Out in the open like that, you'll get the wrong kind of attention. Plus, you got dropped off by a Yellow Tiger patrol car."

Miles had noticed no cameras about the hotel. "The nearest pawn shop, then?"

"Look it up on Seraph net."

"Some places are harder to find and aren't listed. Places with special inventory."

The hotel clerk made a back of the throat sucking sound. Drummed fingers. Miles took out a credit chip. He still had the balance of his Herron-Cauley compensation funds from the train fiasco. He loaded the blank chip with a few credits and slid it under the plastic window.

The clerk pocketed the chip. "Place called Red's Recovery Room. Need directions?"

"No. Do I ask for anyone in particular?"

"I wouldn't know. I no longer frequent establishments like that."

***

"If you pick me up at my hotel, I'll pay you what I owe and buy you breakfast."

Miles sent the text. He browsed for a taxi service, as he wasn't expecting Tristan to respond.

"Be there in five," Tristan texted back.

Ten minutes later, Tristan's three-wheeler came to a stop at the curb. The vehicle appeared to have been tidied up. The rear bed stood empty, and the windshield had been polished.

Miles climbed in. "Red's Recovery Room. Know it?"

"Good morning to you too."

"I thought you'd be hungry and want your money. Let's go there."

"What happened to you? The Yellow Tigers..."

"Wanted to chat, that's all. You're free today? Not planning any more fishing trips?"

"That depends on you giving me my credits."

Miles told him the address of the bar.

Tristan gave a humorless laugh and shook his head. "Now you're taking me to a not-so-pleasant neighborhood before paying me. Why did I even come?"

"Relax. I've been to the good neighborhoods of Seraph. I'm not impressed."

Larger trucks filled the streets as they got closer to their destination. An industrial area, oddly clean compared to River City's factory district. Warehouses, a material yard, workshops, and mechanics were nestled around a bar with a neon sign in a curtained window. Red's, the sign blinked. Faded painted lettering spelled out part of what might be Red's Recovery Room above the door, but it was too sun-bleached to be certain.

Tristan parked across the street and nervously adjusted a strap of his tank top. "I'm guessing there's no dress code."

"I'm sure you'll be underdressed even for this place."

The inside of Red's was dim. Miles paused just past the doorway to let his eyes adjust. Tristan bumped into him. Crimson light burned in a dozen nautilus-shaped sconces. Red's featured six booths and as many small round tables with folding chairs. A white light glowed from behind a tiny window in a swinging back door. The air smelled of lemons. Mellow guitar music played softly from an unseen speaker.

A large man sitting behind the bar glanced up from a tablet. He wore a half-unbuttoned short-sleeved collared shirt and a choker on his neck. A glass of ice water with a wedge of lime sat next to him.

He pressed his hand to a device on the base of his throat. "Help you?" he asked in a mechanical voice.

Miles sat at the corner of the bar. "Serving breakfast?"

The proprietor jerked a thumb at an almost unreadable whiteboard hanging above a credit terminal on the back counter. The Chinese script took Insight a moment to decipher.

"Steamed buns and a green tea and whatever he's having," Miles said.

Tristan nodded at a few of the tap handles. "I'll have the stout."

The proprietor poured a frothy black beer with a white head and let it rest. He ambled to the back door and shouted Miles' breakfast order before returning and topping off the beer.

As soon as he was served, Tristan sipped and nodded appreciatively. "As good as what mother made."

"I'll take your word for it," Miles said. "A bit early for me."

"I don't comment on your fashion choices. You don't get to comment on my diet."

The proprietor returned to his perch atop a stool and resumed scrolling on his tablet.

"I heard this may be a place to buy and sell property," Miles said.

The proprietor put a finger to the mike on what turned out to be a tracheotomy box. "This look like the flea market?"

"This looks like a place with no militia or cameras. I'm looking for a few items. I'm paying a finder's fee." Miles produced his device and turned it so the proprietor could see. Although the images of the stolen figurines weren't clear, it was good enough to tell what they were.

The proprietor turned the volume down on a tiny radio before giving Miles' device his full attention. He squinted. "Impressive, if that's actual gold and real gemstones. Pretty fancy little dancer. Gaudy for my taste."

"We all serve our clients, right?"

"And you—excuse me, your client—is looking to buy not any old precious figurine, but these specifically? This sounds more like a hunt for missing property. This the first place you stopped?"

"Naturally. What other places would you suggest, if not here?"

"Take it easy, partner. Red's is full-service if you have credits."

Miles pulled up his credit app. Showed the screen and his remaining balance.

"That'll do for a finder's fee. That gets you in contact with a seller."

A woman in an apron brought Miles his steamed buns and tea. Miles ate one. It was hot and starchy, but the bean curd filling needed spice. He sipped the tea. It was scalding.

Tristan was almost finished with his beer by the time Miles could try the tea again without blistering his tongue.

Meanwhile, the proprietor was back reading on his tablet. "I've sent a few messages around. Pretty unique items, especially the dancing figurine. Voice activated, if it comes from the same artisan I'm looking at."

"Where's this artisan?"

"Here in town. Does limited production runs of dolls and toys. I'm sure that'll catch a buyer's eye."

"So if someone pawns it off, you'll hear about it."

"That's what your fee pays for. Of course, I might make a bundle reselling it."

"You might. But you won't. Wouldn't want to spoil our budding relationship." Miles filled an empty credit chip and slid it over the bar. "That's a deposit for good faith."

The proprietor plugged the chip into the register. Grunted. "So it is. You'll be contacted once I hear anything."

"Fair enough. And I'll be back either way."

Miles watched the man long enough to see the implied threat sink in. The proprietor nodded amicably as Miles and Tristan turned to leave.

Chapter Nineteen

"So we're hunting for toys now?" Tristan asked as he started the vehicle.

"It's the best lead I have. Someone robbed Beatrix Fish's home and took some of Agatha's collection of treasures. Expensive items. It's something to go on while I think of what else to do."

"There a reward for returning them?"

"Not exactly."

"But Beatrix Fish wants you to follow the trail to her daughter."

"She fired me."

Tristan killed the engine. "So what are we doing here? What am *I* doing here?"

"You're going to drive me to a few pawn shops and we're going to put the word out that we're buyers for jewel-encrusted ballerinas, in case Red or whatever the owner's name is doesn't pull through with his side of our deal."

"Pay me."

"Are you going to drive?"

"Not until I have a credit chip. Credit chip, and then I'll make up my mind."

Once paid, Tristan got them underway. Miles gave him the first address of five registered pawn shops. He wasn't optimistic about any of them, but following the evidence, no matter how thin, was the only thing he knew.

After five minutes, he also knew they were being followed.

An electric motorbike had been behind them since Red's. It hung back most of the time but noticeably sped up whenever they navigated an intersection and encountered any traffic. Single rider, wearing a light gray jumpsuit and full helmet. Miles kept it to himself. Didn't want Tristan to get squirrely.

The bike vanished once they parked in a lot near a couple of the pawn shops. Miles didn't turn up any information on the figurines in either store, and judging by their inventory, none saw any high-end jewelry or rarified collectibles. Plenty of tools, instruments, firearms, appliances, and clothing. He knew he would have to expand his search to actual jewelers.

By noon, he had visited each shop on his list and interviewed two jewelry store managers. The last recognized the ballerina and knew the address of the artisan's place of business. A toy shop.

Tristan's stomach rumbled loud enough that Miles could hear it above the whine of the engine. He looked longingly at a row of food carts near a construction site.

Miles kept his eyes on the road. No need to glance back. He had spotted the bike earlier and didn't want to make a show of watching it. "Probably wishing you had ordered something to eat back at Red's."

"I'm fine. I'm just worried you won't be thinking straight, seeing that it's lunchtime."

"Considerate, aren't you?"

"I know an excellent lunch spot. Best pickles, good curry. Covered rice. Fresh fish. Only cost us a couple of credits."

"I offered breakfast. The rest of your meals are up to you."

Having been a father and boss, he knew tough love was the only way to get children and subordinates to dress up for cold weather and pack their lunch before a shift or a day in school. Let them freeze and starve for a day, and they come through.

***

The toy shop sold automations of all kinds, all frivolous, and everything from shelf-sized figures like the ballerina to full-sized dogs, birds, and cats. The place had several customers with children who were ogling an admittedly remarkable life-sized mockup of a maned lion, which dominated the center of the showroom. The mechanical animal blinked, shook its head as if harassed by flies, and rumbled before settling down as if for a nap. Not bad, Miles reasoned, for an animal he guessed no one in Seraph had ever seen in real life.

"It can run as fast as the real thing," a bespectacled clerk said proudly. "It can also sit, follow, fetch, and even be programmed to keep a schedule."

"Does he talk?" a young girl asked.

The clerk got down on his haunches and offered a warm smile. "If he could, what would you have him say?"

The girl giggled. "He would call my brother a poopy head."

"Clarice," the father said sternly. "Truly remarkable creations, Armen. Everything here is amazing craftsmanship."

"All our stock has their prices listed, at least for those without a deposit. But, ah, I see your dog is finished with its tune up. Call me if you experience any issues."

A shop employee brought out a golden-haired dog with stubby legs and dangling tresses on its ears, which dragged on the floor. The animal yapped as it bounded to the girl, then her brother, licking them both in the face as the father paid the clerk with his device.

Tristan lingered near the entrance as Miles browsed. One side of the showroom was dedicated to more fantastic creations. None were as large as the lion, but lined up in various poses stood dragons, brightly colored horses, teddy bears, a hippogryph, and an adorable rendition of a family of dinosaurs.

Once the family departed, the clerk made a beeline for him. The name Armen was embroidered on his white shirt pocket. "Welcome to the Imaginarium. How can I assist you?"

Miles pulled out his device. "I'm interested in ballerinas. This one in particular."

"Oh, yes. Oh, certainly. That's one of mine. My take on a music box dancer. This one has a strontium battery which will last for decades. Are you looking for a similar build? Each piece is hand crafted and absolutely unique. The casts are custom made, either to your specification or I design it based on whatever input you provide. Looking for a mood? A color? A mockup of a favorite relative? No detail is too small. The music box will also pair with a sound system. An exquisite gift. Some of my clients purchase these as commemoration pieces. I have a catalog of fashions and costumes to choose from. Chinese, Russian, European, even tin-can opera masterworks. Although this piece merely spins, a dancer can be crafted which will emulate any style of performance you desire, including zero-g dance."

"Actually, I'm looking to see if anyone tried to sell this particular ballerina back to you."

Armen made a face as if Miles had just sneezed on him. "Sell it back to me? Whatever for? I honor my warranties if that's your question."

"It isn't. Someone stole this one from Beatrix Fish. Do you know her?"

"Of course I know of her. But I've never met her personally. Am I to understand this dancer was taken from Mrs. Fish?"

"Yeah. A burglar just last night. I'm helping with the investigation and thought I'd try you to see if you heard anything."

"I haven't heard a thing, Mister…"

"Miles Kim."

"You don't appear to be an officer of any militia."

"This is a private inquiry."

Armen composed himself, no doubt deciding if Miles was there representing Beatrix Fish. "To your question, no one has tried to return this or any other of my works recently or ever."

"Yeah, I kind of figured that. I wouldn't think anyone would come straight here. But maybe you know of a second-hand market for high-end toys and jewelry. If someone wanted to move a pricy music box like this, where would they go?"

"I'm sure I wouldn't know."

"At this point, I'll take a guess. I'm sure Mrs. Fish would appreciate any help. Her daughter was quite attached to her ballerina."

Armen sighed and placed a finger against his lips as if in deep thought. "A pawn shop, perhaps? There are also listings for sale items on Seraph net, but I'm sure you've scoured those."

Miles hadn't. "Of course I have. If you think of anything, here's my number."

After providing his information, he tried not to let his disappointment show. If the best Armen could do was direct him back to Seraph's pawn shops, Miles felt he was reaching an end to where the stolen figurines might lead him. And he doubted any thief would be so stupid as to list them in the net's classifieds. What he needed was a decent photo of Agatha. Then he could start the real grunt police work and try to figure out where a young girl might run off to.

"One last thing," Miles said. "Do you have a back exit?"

Chapter Twenty

Tristan hurried to catch up and almost stumbled as they navigated through the Imaginarium's open air back lot. Half-finished projects competed for space with scrap wood, molded plastic, and metal. Several large material printers chugged along under the supervision of a team of toy makers.

A small radio played up-tempo pop music, the volume high enough to be heard above the noise. The radio appeared to be the same or similar model to the others he had seen of late.

No one paid them any mind as they passed through the lot. The workshop's back gate clicked closed behind them, letting them out into an alley between a row of brick buildings.

Device in hand, Tristan paused to look the opposite direction of where they were going. "Hey, my trike is back out on the street."

"I wanted to check something out. The owner told me I might have some luck with one of his neighbors."

"Which one? I'll pull around and we can go in together."

"This way is faster."

He led Tristan through the back alleyways to a sidewalk and scanned it for the motorbike. Didn't see it. After a speeding van zipped past, he darted across the street and headed straight into a café.

"Your lead's in here?"

"Yeah. We can get you your lunch at the same time. Grab us a table. I'll be out back."

The café had a rear exit down a cramped passage with a single restroom. The establishment shared a small weed-infested parking lot with several other neighboring businesses. A recycling bin sat next to a water tank. Miles crouched between them. He only had to wait a minute.

The high whine of the electric bike engine grew louder. The rider pulled up next to the first of the parked cargo vans and glanced about. He tapped a screen on his dashboard. A phone app. Miles couldn't quite make out the conversation, but he didn't need to. He could hear enough to know who the rider was speaking with.

Tristan.

Miles walked straight for the rider. Before he could react, Miles gave him a hard shove, the bike keeling over. The rider scrambled back as Miles advanced and slugged him. The rider sprawled on the ground. Miles was on him as the rider grabbed for a burner. He dropped it when Miles slammed him once, twice, a third time into the concrete. Tore the man's helmet off. Young, early twenties perhaps, frosted spikey white hair, in good shape, eyes wide with fear. Miles prepared to cuff him when the rider went limp.

"S-stop! I give up!"

Miles kept a hand on his chest while patting him down. Beneath the bike jumpsuit, the rider wore a Yellow Tiger militia uniform.

"Why are you following me?"

"I wasn't. I mean, I was, but just to see if you have any leads."

"Leads on what?"

"The Fish girl. Everyone's out looking for her. Lieutenant called in everyone who was off duty. There's a reward."

"So off-duty Yellow Tigers are looking for Agatha. You have a picture?"

"My mobile is on the bike."

Miles let go of him and unclipped the device from the bike's dash. Handed it to the rider. "Share what you have."

The young cop was sitting up. "I'll get in trouble."

Miles gave him his best grumpy cyborg glower. With a few swipes, Agatha's face and physical details popped up on Miles' device. It was the first good look he had of Agatha. Long bangs hid most of her eyes. She wasn't smiling and looked as if she had been cornered by whoever had snapped the picture. She wore a bright dress, and the photo had been taken on a sunny day somewhere outside with a lot of green, perhaps the Fish mansion, or some park, or another home in the swank Woodbine neighborhood.

"So you were following me, hoping that I'd lead you to her?"

"Word's out that you're looking."

"And who's offering the reward?"

The young cop looked confused. "You don't know? Gennady Fish, of course. Lieutenant says find her by whatever means necessary and bring her back to the compound."

"All right. Get out of here. If I see you again, I'm telling Captain Sin and Lieutenant Chati you shared operational details with me."

Miles helped him stand.

The cop picked up his helmet. Hesitated. "Do you have a lead? We've been on the street all night and all morning and no one's seen anything. We could work together, split the reward."

"Scram."

***

Miles found Tristan at the counter inside the café, texting on his phone. Tristan had no food or drink yet. Miles took a seat next to him.

A woman in jeans and a t-shirt with the café logo was finishing busing a nearby table. As she placed the dishes into a bin, she scowled at them. "You and your friend going to order or just take up space?"

Miles glanced at the white board on the wall. "Vegetable curry wrap, spicy, and a water. And whatever he's having."

Tristan pulled the phone close so the screen wasn't visible. "Uh, the same."

She scribbled down a note and vanished into the kitchen.

Miles grabbed a couple of napkins. "Your Yellow Tiger contact won't be following us anymore."

"What do you mean?"

"I sent him packing. Smart, finding someone else who'll pay you if we find the girl. Stupid, because you're fired."

Tristan put his device away and rose.

"You may as well enjoy your lunch. I'll cover you."

"I don't get it."

"You got me this far. I found out what I could. But I've hit a dead end."

He showed Tristan the picture of Agatha. Tristan studied it for a moment before shaking his head.

"You're wondering why I'm doing this," Miles said. "Why go after her if her own mother and father can't get past themselves or each other and find their daughter? Even the cops like the one you were messaging have taken a side. I'm doing it for her."

The server brought water and utensils before bringing menus to an older pair of men who had just entered. Someone dinged a bell in the kitchen. A moment later, Miles and Tristan had their wraps. Spicier than Miles had expected, and he drank all his water by the time he finished and needed a refill.

He paid the server, dabbed his lips, and rose. "Coming?"

"You said I was fired."

"You were. Now I'm offering to rehire you. Same rate as before. You're going to help me find her and bring her home. No more talking to the militia. Let me handle that. And Tristan?"

"Yeah?"

"If you go behind my back again, I'll break your arm."

Chapter Twenty-One

Tristan remained sullen during their drive to a bland section of downtown that held a charity kitchen. From there, Miles intended to check a few shelters and a hostel, but didn't imagine the Yellow Tigers would have missed them if they had been out all night. As Tristan circled in search of street parking, Miles counted twice that a runner with the Yellow Tiger insignia drove past. Then a third went by.

"A lot of cops," Miles said. "This area see much crime?"

"As much as anyplace else in Seraph."

"Word of a reward gets around, I guess, unless there's something else going on. These cops didn't seem this motivated when there was a train full of people that needed rescuing."

Tristan got them parked behind a water tanker truck and switched off the engine. Stared down at the dash as it went dark. "What does it matter if it's you or them?"

"What?"

"What's the difference if you find the girl or they do? The militia will hand her back to her father. You give her to her mother. That's a better shake than most people get, not that I'm saying she's not worth it."

"It's not a perfect answer, but a Seraph court decided Agatha gets to live with her mother. As messed up as her family is, that's where Agatha belongs. If her dad wants her, then let him go through proper channels. All he's accomplishing now is raising the chances that his daughter gets hurt by some idiot with a burner wanting to be the one who brings her back. And if it wasn't for him, she might never have left home in the first place."

Tristan grunted and didn't get out of the wagon with Miles.

"You going to be here when I return?" Miles asked.

"I'll be here. That spicy curry wrap isn't sitting well."

"Suit yourself."

***

Miles spent over an hour in and around the charity kitchen, showing Agatha's picture to anyone who didn't run away from him. The kitchen played a sermon throughout, but Miles tuned it out, getting into the almost forgotten groove of canvasing for eyewitnesses. Most folks were friendly. The Yellow Tigers had already asked some of them about the girl. The kitchen staff had placed a picture of her on their door just that morning, right next to the donation terminal and a vending machine which offered free radios.

No one had seen her.

Miles hadn't remembered this many people in need of help in River City. While he and his family had lived on or near the base, it was rare to see anyone who the social services couldn't help. Not so with Seraph.

Tristan was waiting for him as promised.

They drove to the shelters. Already saw each had their picture of Agatha in their doors. So did the hostel. The militia had the word out and was moving faster than Miles could have imagined.

"Aren't you getting out?" Tristan asked.

"Yellow Tigers got here first. I can't compete with their manpower. Maybe Beatrix has the names of Agatha's friends, anyone who might help hide her when running away..."

"But you got yourself fired."

Miles nodded as he scanned the passing faces. Someone, somewhere, always knew something. The useless bromide got repeated in the serials so often it must have been a joke among police officers for generations. But it didn't mean it wasn't true.

Tristan merged with the traffic. "I'll start driving. We keep our eyes open. Maybe we see something."

Miles gave him a go-ahead gesture and watched the street without focusing on where they were going. A broad sandy lot near a house-sized dwarf reactor had scores of stalls and blankets spread with wares. A modest crowd browsed the flea market, picking through produce, clothes, tools, vehicle parts, and packaged food products.

"Stop here."

Miles got out and walked through the rows of wares and junk. He didn't show Agatha's picture and didn't speak to anyone. Marveled at what they would put up for sale, including old bedrolls, stained clothing, and a jar of used toothbrushes. He knew he had been naïve in his search. If Agatha was just wandering Seraph, she'd be found by now. But if she had slipped away from her father, she had a place to go. And if not with a friend, then someone had lured her away.

He returned to Tristan's three-wheeler. "We're going back to Beatrix Fish's home."

Tristan got them underway. Almost spoke a few times but held back.

"You're wondering why," Miles said. "We need to know who Agatha's friends are, who she talked to on the net, and anything about other family they haven't mentioned who might take her in. Schoolmates. Neighbors. Even former employees she might have been fond of."

"I'm sure the militia asked those questions. Mrs. Fish won't share that with you, would she?"

Miles let the question linger. If Beatrix won't share, then perhaps Kitty would. Or Celia. It was always harder to stonewall someone when they showed up in person. And Miles wasn't ready to give up. Plus, there was the possibility he had missed something about the burglary. A list of party guests would be helpful. While he was at it, maybe Beatrix Fish would give him a foot rub.

As they turned into a roundabout, four militia bikes pulled up alongside and behind them. One of the bikers didn't have his helmet on. It was the spikey haired young man Miles had waylaid by the café.

"Get us out of here," Miles said.

A sharp electric crackle, and the three-wheeler went dead. An electromagnetic disabler, Miles knew. Tristan got them pulled over with their remaining momentum. The cops stopped around them and dismounted from their bikes. They had their hands on the butts of their sidearms. Spikey Hair approached his side of the vehicle.

Miles placed his palms on the dashboard. "How can we cooperate with the militia this fine afternoon?"

Spikey Hair grinned. "Seems you're interfering with Seraph militia business."

"We're not interfering with anything or anyone."

"Showing Agatha Fish's picture around? Assaulting an officer? And I learned you're supposed to be in a cell on hold back at the station. We've got plenty of grounds to not only detain you but to bust your head."

He slid a truncheon from his belt. Two others did the same, while the fourth drew his burner.

"Step out of the vehicle," Spikey Hair said.

Miles glanced at Tristan. Tristan's lips trembled and he was bathed in sweat. "I didn't...I didn't call..."

"It's all right. They're here for me. Okay, ladies and gentlemen, for the record, I'm cooperating. I have a burner on my belt. I'd like to remove it and place it on the floor."

"I said step out of the vehicle," Spikey Hair said. "Hands raised. Do not lower them."

Miles climbed out of the three-wheeler. None of the cops appeared to want to get close and were waiting on Spikey Hair.

"We cuffing him?" the cop with the drawn pistol asked.

Spikey Hair sneered. "Too much trouble. Captain Sin might just cut him loose again. But we can teach a lesson. Just don't hurt him too badly, not that anyone could tell with that face of his."

It was at that moment Insight targeted the four cops. The aim assist dropped a square on each face, with a secondary light circle appearing center-mass. At this range, he couldn't miss, if he only had his weapon out. His artificial arm and hand could snap off four clean shots within a second. Of course, he'd be dead too.

"He's targeting us!" Spikey Hair said.

The other three cops drew their sidearms. Miles kept frozen, his hands above his head, and tried to switch Insight off. Double blink. Double blink. It wasn't responding.

"Insight off. Insight off. I'm not targeting anyone. I'm surrendering."

His module suggested additional targets: the cop's weapons, their exposed hands, the gaps in their armor, the potentially explosive batteries on their bikes.

INSIGHT OFF!

The sharp mental command did the trick. The target reticles vanished. But he had four burner barrels aiming at him. It was a wonder none of the cops had fired.

Miles licked his lips. "It's off. My module is off. We all want the same thing. Bring the girl home. It's what your captain wants. I'm not getting in your way. You have no reason to get in mine."

One cop threw him to the ground. Another removed his burner from his belt. Sharp pain as they twisted his arms behind his back. One was kneeling on top of him as another made a quick search of the three-wheeler. The third cop was getting Tristan out from behind the steering wheel. Tristan was gripping it as if his life depended on it.

"I'm just a ride for hire!" Tristan mewled.

Tristan was shoved against the hood and patted down. Once the cop zip tied him, the militiaman came back around to stand over Miles. The burners got holstered. The truncheons came out again. The three appeared to be waiting on Spikey Hair. Miles didn't see any rank insignia, but bullies had their own pecking order.

Chatter crackled over their helmet radios.

Spikey Hair replied, "Lance 16 copy. Yes. We're detaining a potential witness—copy that. It's the ex-cop you were so upset about. Me and my lance, we can—copy that, too, sir." After a long pause, he put his weapon away and glared at Miles. "It's your lucky day. Saddle up, boys. We'll revisit this another time. The search is over. The Lieutenant wants everyone back at the station. We found the girl."

Chapter Twenty-Two

"She's safe."

Celia said this with a deadpan expression that Miles couldn't penetrate. He tapped the tablet screen and watched the thirty-second video again. There was Agatha. She was busy doodling at the desk in the bedroom of her father's house, her dark hair tied back, her face intent on whatever she was drawing.

The perspective changed, with Gennady Fish now occupying the screen. "As you can see, Beatrix, our girl is fine. She was hiding out at Samantha's and was up in her tree house. She said she didn't want to go home just yet. She got scared when the militia showed up to see her and talk to me. I'm sure she'll get bored and want to come back. Let's give her a couple of days."

The video froze. Miles stood at the doorway to the Fish mansion. An overcast haze filled the sky and light sprinkles fell on the roundabout. Each droplet evaporated on the paving stones in moments. Tristan remained seated within his three-wheeler and was watching cautiously through the windshield, as if at any moment a fresh squad of cops was going to boil out through the front door and accost them.

Celia took the tablet back. "You see, Mr. Kim? Thank you for your concern. I'm sure Mrs. Fish is likewise grateful."

"I'm sure she is. I'm also sure she's not happy Agatha isn't coming home yet."

"You are correct; she is furious. But for now, at least we know Agatha has been found and is with her father."

"He sent this video?"

"Yes. Mrs. Fish doesn't accept his calls."

Kitty appeared behind the maid. She was dressed in a formal riding suit, with a red blazer, white pants, and a black round helmet with a short bill. "Now Celia, Mother's not listening. At least for Miles' last report, we can tell him the truth."

She edged past Celia and showed a tablet with a split screen. On either side of the divide, Gennady and Beatrix Fish were talking, but the sound was muted.

"Mother doesn't like the staff to admit that she and Gennady chat. Sometimes they do more than talk. It's an off and on duel, with the occasional fling.

It's love your enemy and hate your neighbor, but it's okay if you let him in for the occasional dipsy-doodle so long as he doesn't stay for breakfast."

"You're able to eavesdrop on their conversation?" Miles asked.

Kitty showed her teeth when she grinned. "What fun would it be if I missed this?"

She unmuted the tablet.

"...have no right, Gennady," Beatrix said. "She belongs here. This is her home. She needs her mother."

"And she'll come back to the house," Gennady answered. "Give her some time. She's upset. You know how she gets. I don't want to see her have another episode."

"Then I'm coming there. I'm bringing Doctor Varner. He'll give her a shot and then there won't be any fuss."

"Dr. Varner has been by. You can call him."

"He's not your doctor!" Beatrix said, her voice trembling.

"He's not yours, either! He's Agatha's and if you—"

Kitty muted it. "Five...four...three...two...uh, almost. No, yes, I'm right. They're done. Mom hung up. She never lasts long once she breaks and her voice cracks. This is one for the record book."

"So your sister is okay?" Miles asked.

"You saw the footage. She's peachy."

"I saw the footage. So what's wrong with her?"

"Nothing a doctor can't charge for, year in, year out. Treat her, let her blood, have her swallow her medicine, and wring their hands when she takes a turn."

"So she's sick."

"You saw the video. She's as right as rain."

"Kitty, there you are," Beatrix Fish said as she came hurrying down the stairs. "Mr. Kim, I should have you arrested. You've wasted my time and re-sources."

Celia bowed and backed away, and Kitty's grin only widened as she made space for her mother at the doorway.

Miles held his ground. "Maybe I wasted some of your time. But Kitty showed me the video. It looks like your daughter is okay."

"This is a disaster! I wanted her home, quietly, not to be held hostage."

"If you're worried about your ex hurting her, then we can go together and collect her."

"I won't set foot in his house."

"I visited Gennady's place. He's got his goons there. He's got the militia out to get me. People don't do that unless they're hiding something. But now we have proof of where Agatha is. We talk to Captain Sin of the Yellow Tigers, and we bring Agatha home."

Beatrix fixed him with a frosty gaze. It was the look one gave a cockroach in the sink. "This isn't your concern. You failed, and yet you keep turning up. I should call my lawyer about you, but I imagine you have nothing I can threaten you with. But you're not welcome here at my house. It would be best you leave Seraph and crawl back inside whatever hole you climbed out of. Celia, the door. And if Mr. Kim doesn't drive that heap of junk out the gate in the next minute, call the militia."

Chapter Twenty-Three

The cargo containers made up a sprawling neighborhood on the west side of Seraph.

Makeshift shelters stood sandwiched between the plastic and steel boxes. Sagging tarps pitter-pattered with drops as the rain grew heavy. Desperate gardens grew in buckets, bins, and raised planter boxes made of scrap. Peppers, tomatoes, and beans obscured the entrance to a shanty, where a dusty blanket decorated with smiling cartoon chickens and rabbits served as a door.

Tristan pulled the three-wheeler up so that it was partially covered by a sheet metal overhang. "Mi casa es su casa."

"Why are we here?" Miles asked.

"Because you didn't tell me where you wanted to go after I asked three times. Come on."

Miles followed him inside and was surprised by the size of the front room. The floor had heavy rugs laid down across it. A makeshift chimney of crimped steel scraps served an iron stove and ran up into a hole cut in the ceiling. A tea pot simmered. Bundles of electric cords were draped high on one wall, the lines splitting off and providing current to a refrigerator, an electric oven, and a few lamps set on the floor, all by the grace of an overloaded power strip.

A very pregnant woman in a flower pattern sundress stirred from a plush beanbag chair. Tristan leaned in to kiss her.

"Honey, this is my employer, Miles. Miles, this is Yasmin."

The woman put on glasses. "Welcome to our home."

Tristan helped her rise and got her seated at a rickety table on an even more wobbly resin chair that looked like it would bend, break, or both at the slightest provocation. He then went to fix a pot of tea. He made a show of examining a set of cups waiting in a drying rack next to a basin of sudsy water.

He placed a handful of loose leaves into the teapot. "Have a seat, Miles."

Miles checked the chair next to Yasmin and confirmed it was equally flimsy. He leaned to examine a set of metal shelves propped up on glass blocks. Framed printed photos lined the top shelf. Tristan and Yasmin together, one standing by a canyon with an expansive view, another of them frolicking in a sapphire lake, and a third picture of them wearing helmets, heavy shirts, and slacks, with picks and shovels in hand, and covered head to toe in dirt. They posed alongside a crew of ten before a massive excavator.

"Construction crew?" Miles asked.

Yasmin leaned forward and fought to get comfortable. "Platinum mine. Back when the surface-level easy pickings were drying up. You could make a good haul, if you put in the hours. But then our co-op got bought out and our manager skipped off with the proceeds."

"You didn't stick with it?"

"Corporate mines wanted long contracts and used some nasty chemicals. Tristan got sick. So we quit and tried some other things."

"Like fishing," Tristan said with a laugh.

Miles crouched to examine a polished chunk of ore that sparkled with crystals. "When are you due?"

"The fourth of next month," Yasmin said. "I pray it will be a day late or a day early."

"My honey is superstitious," Tristan said. "As if we didn't have our share of bad luck already. I keep telling her that luck, good and bad, runs its course and changes. It always does. It always will."

"You can't be too careful," Yasmin said. "But unlike Tristan, I don't believe things have to change. Sometimes a trajectory keeps going up or down unless you stop it. What do you believe, Miles?"

Miles put the ore back and sat at the table. "I think you're both lucky to have each other. Any other family to help out?"

Yasmin and Tristan made eye contact. Both smiled.

"We're going to be fine," Yasmin said. "Get the yuca cake, dear. Unless you ate it all."

Tristan poured the tea before going to the refrigerator and bringing out a half-empty rectangular pan of something that looked custardy with a bottom crust. With a spatula, he served Miles and Yasmin a square.

Miles looked at the offering suspiciously.

"Use your fingers," Yasmin prompted. "You don't have any allergies, do you?"

"None that I pay any attention to." He sampled the pastry and found it shockingly sweet but edible. The tea was cool enough to sip, and it washed down some of the syrupy flavor.

"Tristan is driving for you today. Will there be more work for him tomorrow?"

"Afraid not. We were both let go."

"That's too bad. It sounds like you will have to start your own search for work. Tristan says you had a wealthy client."

"A little too wealthy. Doesn't know what to do with it all, if you ask me. We were looking for her daughter. But the daughter wasn't missing, just at a friend's house. Now that she's turned back up, the job's done."

Yasmin nibbled at her pastry. "If only all things were that simple."

Miles took out his device and his last empty credit chip. He had been given enough from Herron-Cauley to make ends meet for a short while. He transferred the balance to the chip and placed it on the table next to Yasmin.

"That squares us."

Yasmin pocketed the chip without checking it. Tristan stood by her side and was eating his own piece of yuca cake with his fingers.

When Miles got up, Tristan flinched. His eyes kept darting. "I can give you a ride back to your hotel."

"It's okay. I'll walk it."

"It's raining out, Miles," Yasmin said. "And there's no hotel near here."

"I won't rust much. It'll be a chance for me to clear my head. I hope something turns up, work wise, for you, Tristan. And Yasmin? I hope you love and care for that kiddo in your belly."

"We will. And it's kiddos. Twins. Boy and girl, if the obstetrician is correct."

He made it outside and squinted as the sun shone down from a gap between black clouds. The rain was a thick mist. Then his phone rang.

"This is Red. You were by my place looking for some property to show. Well, it looks like it has. A ballet dancer music box? One of my vendors tagged it after I shared the picture."

"Oh yeah? Where is it now?"

"All in good time. You said something about a finder's fee. You give that, and you get a location. As a bonus, I'll share with you the camera footage of the guy who just came in to sell it. Happened just a few minutes ago. And he had a little girl with him. Same girl as the one the militia was asking about earlier. This worth something to you?"

Chapter Twenty-Four

"Will apologizing help?"

Tristan ignored Miles' question. He had remained dour during the drive back to the industrial zone and Red's Recovery Room. The shouting match that had erupted between Tristan and Yasmin had been loud enough that their neighbors in the other cargo containers had stuck their heads out their doors.

Miles waited in the cab of the three-wheeler. His request would either be met or he'd need a backup plan. But when Tristan hurried outside, he slipped behind the wheel and handed Miles his credit chip back.

Tristan pulled in front of Red's. "Tell me again there's a payday at the end of this."

"A good chance of one."

"You said nothing about a chance before."

"I needed those credits back. I wouldn't ask if it wasn't an emergency. You'll get paid."

"I'm putting my neck on the line with this. What makes you so certain Red, or whoever this guy is, is telling the truth?"

"I can't risk assuming otherwise."

"You don't have a gun."

"They rarely help. Are you sitting here or coming inside?"

Red's had more customers at midafternoon. The bar and half the tables were occupied, and the music coming from the speaker was louder and playing something twangy sung in Spanish.

The proprietor was finishing pouring a beer. He served it to a woman in a frumpy silk suit before pointing Miles and Tristan at a corner booth.

"You have some information for me," Miles said.

Red wedged himself onto the bench opposite them and pushed on his tracheotomy box to speak. "Like I said on the phone. Buyer picked up one of your items. Also, got a picture of your girl."

"Let me see."

Red gave him a long look before pulling out his device and swiping until he had a still from an overhead security camera. There was Agatha Fish standing next to a bearded man in a long-sleeved garment with a pushed-back hood. The image was grainy enough that Miles thought the garment might be leather, but it looked like a rain suit. The man's beard was long and braided several times, and he had a head of long locks. And at his side, Agatha appeared to be nestled up against him as he stood at the counter. Time stamp: twenty-four minutes ago.

Unless Agatha had a twin sister, this was her. Which meant the Agatha in Gennady Fish's video was as fake as the Agatha at the mansion ball.

"And where was this?" Miles asked.

"Let's have that finder's fee."

"The dancing figurine isn't what I'm interested in. The girl's not safe."

"Not my problem. And this isn't a charity. I have my own bills to pay. If you're not here to do business, then don't waste my time. I'll find a buyer for this information."

Miles didn't want to risk calling Red on a possible bluff. Someone like Gennady Fish would have enemies. Someone else would come through as a new buyer. If Agatha was still in the wind, it was more than likely that the search for her was still on, and that Gennady had given Beatrix enough proof to get his ex to calm down. But from Miles' perspective, Agatha's father was more motivated in saving face in his efforts to find his girl.

Seeing the strange man with the girl made Miles' stomach tighten.

He handed Red the credit chip. "This gets me in contact with the shop owner?"

Red checked the chip. "This isn't the agreed-upon amount."

"You're shy the price of lunch. Give me a break."

"You trying to lowball me is a waste of my time." He collected his device.

"This isn't me lowballing. It's a fair price. It's also all I have. Me finding her is that important."

"Then get a job with social services."

Tristan fumbled with the pockets of his vest and pulled out a credit stick. "I have it."

Red scanned it, grunted, and drained both sticks of their funds and then passed his device around for a thumb scan. He then sent Miles an address. Vittorio's Pawn and Loan.

"Nice doing business with you," Red said.

Tristan didn't get up when Miles did. "Wait, what about my change?"

"Call it a fee for exclusive content. Because it seems there might be others interested in knowing what you boys just learned."

Chapter Twenty-Five

They drove towards Vittorio's Pawn and Loan. It had been one of the shops on Miles' list not far from the charity kitchen. Tristan darted in and out of lanes between the larger trucks and swerved hard enough that Miles clung to the seat and the lip of the window simultaneously.

"How much did you give him?" Miles asked.

"Enough to make the difference. That's what matters to you, right?"

"This is my job, not yours. You have someone to care for. Three someones soon."

"And you promised a payday. I'm holding you to that. Because we just got hosed in there."

"Fair enough—watch it!"

Dodging a delivery dog almost took them into the back end of a limo. The three-wheeler missed the rear fender by centimeters as they zipped past on the shoulder and scraped a curb when taking the next corner.

"We have to survive to finish this," Miles said. "Slow down."

Tristan nodded. Blinked hard. Wiped sweat from his eyes. Let off on the accelerator.

"Lot of responsibility bringing a kid into the world," Miles said casually.

"You have children?"

"I'm not all machine. I have a son. I came to Seraph to see him."

"Except now you're doing this."

"I'm going to make sure you get paid."

Tristan laughed. "Yeah, you'd better. Otherwise I don't dare come home."

The rain had left puddles on the thirsty ground. Patches of black water pooled in the gutters. Enough mist descended from the sky to spatter the three-wheeler's windshield. The single wiper wasn't working. Tristan occasionally reached out and wiped the grime and water away, but appeared to be able to see where he was going through the streaks.

Vittorio's Pawn and Loan was a free-standing building on a lot next to a construction project. A foundation lay on the neighboring property, but no one was working. A material handler and a bulldozer hunkered in the weather.

Children were out splashing in the puddles. They parted as the three-wheeler puttered into one of the parking spots next to a desert runner.

"Why don't you wait here?" Miles said.

A bell rang as he entered the shop. A man in a duster and broad hat was looking at a burner as the shopkeeper watched. The shopkeeper was bald, the same man from the video who had purchased the mechanical dancer.

"Be with you in a minute," the shopkeeper said.

Two more burners sat on the counter before the customer. He inspected each, checking the charge and sighting down the barrel at a mounted set of deer antlers up on the wall. The walls were replete with clocks, guitars, decorative long arms, and gaudy paintings of people Miles didn't recognize. He glanced at display cases full of rings, watches, and jeweled chains. Among the treasures were ruby pins, broaches, and even gold teeth.

The shopkeeper's voice carried. "All serious offers considered."

Miles glanced up and saw the shopkeeper was addressing him before returning his attention to his original customer.

Several signs repeated the admonitions: All Sales are Final! Credit Available! Reasonable Rates!

The back of the store had more artistic pieces. Gilded vases, figurines, a thumb-sized owl automaton that opened its eyes when Miles leaned in to inspect it. Next to it stood a platinum statuette of a wispy woman with a turquoise sarape. She appeared to be dancing or about to be swept away by a strong wind.

Miles checked the price tag. Realized he needed a payday soon if he was about to start collecting objets d'art.

The bell jingled as the first customer departed. The shopkeeper was putting away all three burners.

"No sale today?" Miles asked.

"He'll be back. Anyone who tries to bargain that hard on price but doesn't walk sooner always returns. So, is there something I can show you? Fifteen percent off all watches this week. You have an empty holster asking to be filled? I'll give you the price he was asking for on the big ten-shot Harker model I've got here."

"I'm interested in music boxes."

The bald man cinched up his face. "I've got a few. In fact, one just came in that I haven't priced out yet, but it's a real collector's piece. If you want something for a lady friend, the more reasonable items are on that wall."

"I'm searching for something built locally. The Imaginarium. Always been a fan."

"Never mind that wall, then. But if you don't mind me saying, their pieces command a rarified price."

"And you don't think I have the credits."

The bald man shrugged. "I don't go insulting my customers like that. But if I had one of theirs, I wouldn't need to put it out and wait for someone to come browsing."

"Red sent me."

"I guessed as much. You know his name's not really Red."

Miles produced his device and pulled up the picture. "Our relationship didn't progress to the point of formal introductions. Who's this man?"

"A client. Which means it's difficult for me to remember his particulars, seeing as how I wouldn't have a business if I shared that kind of information with anyone who comes in asking."

"I don't care about your client or what he's into. I'm not a cop, I'm not militia, I'm just interested in having a conversation with him."

Miles drummed his metal fingers on the top of the glass case. *Rat-tat-tat. Rat-tat-tat.*

"Don't scratch that," the shopkeeper said.

"Wouldn't dream of it. But you know those older servos and neural triggers. Machines get flaky after enough time in the meat, if you know what I mean."

Miles' arm slammed down with a *WHACK!* The glass case spiderwebbed.

The shopkeeper pointed towards the door. "Hey! Get out of here—"

Miles gently took the man's hand as if caressing it. "Newer builds don't have the same problem as some of the ones which saw service during the war. Enhanced defaults that restrict the kPa of applicable pressure unless certain mental checks are given."

"Let go."

Miles adjusted his grip and leaned closer. "Can't have a cyborg accidentally breaking a bed while asleep, or hurting someone during the throes of passion, or, as I can attest to, squeezing something that shouldn't be squeezed during a seizure. Old models and old brains degrade with age. Part of life, really. Motor cortex gets confused sometimes. Doesn't even have to be during a fit or while sleeping. In my case, it could be a lack of concentration. If I get distracted, say. Or upset."

"Look, take the ballerina. Take the burner. I've got credits in my safe."

"Red already taxed me beyond anything I was expecting to pay to get here. I'm out of credits. I'm not asking for you to give me anything. Just a lead on your customer. A name. And anything you can remember about the girl he was with."

The shopkeeper tried to work up spit in his mouth so he could speak. "The girl?"

Was this the only person in Seraph who had missed the memo about Agatha?

"Yeah, the girl."

"I don't know either of them. I swear. He comes in here once in a while with a watch or ring. Always cheap stuff. He never haggles. No chit-chat. Takes my first offer. An easy mark."

"Name?"

The shopkeeper's hand was slick with sweat. "He doesn't give it and I don't ask. I didn't even look at the girl. I take pills in the morning, and I was pretty high when they came in. I'm still coming down off that, and I'm starting to freak out a little. Come on..."

"He didn't say where he got the ballerina? And you weren't at least a little curious how a low-profit customer landed something that was obviously stolen."

"You're in a pawn shop! Half of everything is probably stolen. Everyone's selling something they're trying to move quick. Girlfriends clean out their cheating boyfriends' belongings? Marriage on the rocks and a mate doesn't want to wait for a lawyer to tell them what half of what is theirs? They come here."

Miles applied enough pressure to get the man's attention. "What was the guy's relationship with the girl?"

"How should I know? She was clinging to him like she was scared. If he's some pervo you want to bust, more power to you. If I had a name, I'd give it to you. He's a scrubby waster. Looks like one of those soup kitchen types. Check there, I don't know. The guy's probably a head waster tripping on shabu."

"Why would you think that?"

"Because every time he comes in here with some knick-knack, he also gives me one of those stupid free radios the Church of the Sands whackos hand out, pre-tuned to their broadcasts. I have a basket of them for a couple of credits a piece, not that anyone needs to buy one."

"Show me."

The shopkeeper rubbed his hand as he brought a basket of card-sized radios out from under the counter. "Take one. On the house."

Miles inspected one of the radios. He had seen enough of them to realize this was a popular model, the same as the type the soup kitchen gave away in the vending machine. But something about the radio nagged him, something he had missed. He reviewed the Insight images of Agatha's room. One of the radios had been on her desk at the mansion, and it had been tuned to an evangelist broadcast. A cheap free radio in the room of a little girl whose parents only got her, in Kitty Fish's words, the best?

"That's it," the shopkeeper said. "That's everything. I can't tell you anything else."

"I have another question. How much for that burner?"

"Y-you said you were out of credits."

"I am. But once I make some, I might be back to make a purchase."

Chapter Twenty-Six

They sat parked in the shade of a wilted elm on a side street near the charity kitchen. Miles had made his rounds here already. Asking about Agatha again wouldn't produce any results. Using Insight, he brought up what information he could about the place off Seraph net.

Menu. Hours. A few pictures of happy disadvantaged locals eating. Food and credit donation opportunities. Volunteers needed. A mission statement, an inclusive beacon of hope in the community providing comfort and material giving, blah-blah-blah.

Miles respected the hardworking individuals who put themselves on the line to help others. But in his experience, there was always a catch. Although he had heard nothing onerous in the snippets of church talk pouring from the speakers inside the dining room, forced conversion, rice Christians, and giving with strings attached were concepts as old as man. Giving meant someone at the top of the charity food chain would benefit, even if they balanced the books to show the accountants they were a force for good.

Seo Yeun had accused him of being a cynical son of a bitch on more than one occasion.

"What's the play?" Tristan asked.

"I need to ask better questions. Focus on the man Agatha was with. Someone has to know him."

"And maybe don't look like a bedraggled cop looking to bust someone?"

Miles filed bedraggled away next to feckless. "Yeah. That means you're coming with me to soften my image."

Music played inside, a solo unplugged guitar plucking softly at a blues number over the sound system. The kitchen itself was empty except for a man wiping down tables and straightening chairs. Bangs and clatters came from the partially visible kitchen in the back. Vapor rose from the steam tables, but no dishes had been set in the steel wells. No doubt dinner was being prepared. The air smelled of spices and savory, a rich earthy aroma that recalled a childhood soup his mother would cook when they lived in Jupiter's orbit before joining the reverse exodus back to Earth.

Past the door, an exposed concrete wall displayed a score of child's paintings of flowers, birds, and sunsets.

The man who was tidying up scraped a few chairs along as he dragged them into place. "Not open until five."

"We're not here for supper. My friend and I are here to find out about volunteering."

"Oh, that's excellent. I'm Valentino, one of the assistant managers."

"Miles. A pleasure. We just got settled locally and are looking for a way to give back. We find the message you preach comforting."

"Not my message. But it plays on the radio at the top of each hour. Either of you know your way around a kitchen? Or how to handle guests in a dining room?"

"I'm a back of the house kind of guy."

"Don't be shy. We have a few old timers who frequent us, and we need a variety of faces who know how to be friendly and firm. If either of you are licensed therapists, that would be a boon." Valentino smiled at Tristan. "And what about you, friend?"

"I'm Tristan."

"Tristan here knows a thing or two about fish," Miles said.

"I'm sure your help will be welcome. We don't get enough fish, but when we do, it's a hit. Mostly plant-based foodstuffs here. We own a few greenhouses, and we receive donations."

"What about services?"

"You mean the church? Besides playing their radio program, we don't openly proselytize to our guests. Receive free, give free. We direct folks to several non-denominational outreach programs for aid, but most are secular with no church affiliations."

"I was talking to a bearded man and was hoping maybe I could work with him."

Valentino cocked his head. "Couple of employees with beards."

"This guy had a long one. A head full of locks. Wore a heavy garment with a hood, despite the heat."

"Who are you?"

"Just a concerned neighbor looking to help his brothers and sisters in need."

Valentino let out a sigh and sagged. "We've had enough cops coming through here today asking questions. And I thought you looked familiar. You were around earlier asking questions. No one here's seen Agatha Fish. If she shows up, we'll call the police. You don't need to dangle a reward for anyone here to do what's right. If she ran away, then she needs help and should be reunited with her parents. It's an unkind world out there. So if that's all, then I need to get back to work."

"This guy with the beard was the last person seen with Agatha. He may have her. If his description fits anyone you know, I need you to tell me."

"You've seen our clients. Some aren't the best groomed. You described several of them. But I can't have you here harassing people just looking for a meal."

"That's why I prefer to talk to you," Miles said. "I don't want to waste anyone's time, but this is urgent. This guy's beard had braids. Not a look I've seen around here."

Tristan tapped one of the drawings. "Kind of like this guy?"

In the middle row of the children's drawings along the wall, a brown and yellow thick-lined smudgy watercolor showed a man with a beard with his arms outstretched. The beard looked like a noose around the man's neck. He wore a hood. A plastic plaque in the center of the art display read Anthem Primary School.

Miles tugged the drawing off the wall. Scanned it. The drawing was too rough for a decisive match, but it was enough of a similarity that it couldn't be dismissed.

"What's the relationship between this kitchen and the school?" Miles asked.

Valentino hesitated. "The children are taught the value of assisting those with less than them."

"And?"

"We both receive funding and volunteers from the Church of the Sands."

Spikey Hair and his three goons shoved past a pair of early birds waiting just outside the door. Two of them spread out into the dining room as Spikey Hair and one of the cops headed straight for Miles.

"Case closed, Miles Kim," Spikey Hair said. "I heard you got the message. Yet here you are, beating the street." He snatched the drawing from Miles' hand. "I'm guessing you're not looking to buy art for your crappy hotel room."

"Why are my activities of any interest to you? Agatha's home with her father."

"Yeah, that's what the captain told the rank and file. Back to traffic duty. Got a report of a three-wheel tuk-tuk driving recklessly. Consider this a sobriety check. Let's step outside."

Miles blocked the nearest militia man from laying a hand on Tristan. "No one's drunk. And you didn't receive any call. How about telling me why you're really here in this kitchen. You were following us."

Spikey Hair grinned. "That old robot eye of yours doesn't miss much, does it?"

"Trust me, it misses most things. But your bikes weaving in and out between trucks to keep up with us? Hardly subtle."

"Thought it be a real time saver to let you do our leg work. Because the rest of the department is stumped." He pulled his burner. "Step against the wall. And Valentino, is it? How about you explain what you and Miles were discussing before we entered."

Valentino's hands went up. "They were asking about the girl. I told them what I told the other officers. We haven't seen her."

"But he's interested in your art installation."

"A potential witness who saw the girl."

Spikey Hair showed the rough drawing to the cop next to him, an older trooper with red sideburns. Sideburns nodded.

"You recognize him, don't you?" Miles asked.

Spikey Hair's eyes narrowed. "You say this guy's a witness? That doesn't track. What's the connection between this guy and Agatha Fish?"

"Tell me why you're still asking and we can swap information like civil folk."

He dropped the drawing and aimed his burner at Miles' face. "This isn't a negotiation."

Before the day started, Miles wouldn't have guessed that a Seraph militia cop would shoot down someone in cold blood during an interrogation. But now he wasn't sure.

Miles said, "They were seen together in a pawn shop hawking one of the stolen items from the Fish mansion. And you know Agatha's not really home with her father."

"Aren't you a bright old man? But you also won't go home after being fired. And we don't have time to process an arrest."

Valentino placed a hand on Spikey Hair's weapon, as if to lower the barrel. "Look, officer, I don't want any trouble in here. Mr. Kim shared what he asked me—"

Spikey Hair smashed him in the forehead with the barrel of his pistol. With the burner no longer in his face, Miles didn't hesitate. He grabbed Spikey Hair's arm, twisted, and heard a pop at the wrist as the militia man screamed and dropped his burner. He then fixed his grip on the wriggling man.

The other three backed away while drawing their sidearms.

"Let him go!" Sideburns said.

Miles pulled him close and clamped his right hand on Spikey Hair's throat. The trooper began mewling.

"Tristan, grab the burner."

Without hesitation, Tristan stooped to pick up the dropped pistol.

Miles adjusted his grip on the cop. "Okay. Now tell your men to back off. You and I are stepping outside."

"You're dead," Spikey Hair spat.

"You're probably right. Move or I break something else that won't heal with a regenerator."

He inched his hostage towards the door, with Tristan in the lead. Tristan held the door open and they went outside.

"Who's still looking for Agatha?" Miles asked. When Spikey Hair didn't instantly answer, Miles squeezed.

Spikey Hair groaned. "Our lance. A couple of others."

The three cops were pointing their weapons at him from the opposite side of the glass. Miles kept Spikey Hair as a shield.

"Who else?"

"Gah! All right. Lieutenant Chati has us looking. The girl's worth a fortune. Gennady Fish will pay anything to get her back. That's why you're here, smart guy. Same with us."

Miles held out his free hand to Tristan. Tristan gave him the burner. Miles fired twice into the glass, targeting a table just past the cops. The cops dove for cover and were out of sight for the moment. Spikey Hair was kicking now.

Miles dragged him to the corner before flinging him down. The four bikes were parked at the curb. Insight gave him a target on the four batteries.

Snap! Snap! Snap! Snap!

Green flame and sparks erupted from the bikes.

Miles pushed Tristan towards the three-wheeler, keeping low. Miles expected that at any moment a barrage of laser fire was going to come their way. But as Tristan got them puttering forward, he glanced back. Spikey Hair was alone and struggling to stand. He had his hand to his throat mike and was undoubtedly calling in for backup.

Tristan banged the steering wheel. "What did you do? What did *we* do?"

"What we had to. Watch the road. Straight on Richards Drive, then take a left at the foundry."

"I thought you didn't know your way around town."

"I'm learning quick."

Chapter Twenty-Seven

The Church of the Sands was a boxy structure of faux rough-hewn limestone with the appearance of a fort rather than a place of worship. No spire or steeple, and no decorations adorned the building. A few beds of withered, viny shrubs grew up the front wall but appeared to be losing the struggle against the relentless climate.

"Park around the back," Miles said.

Tristan puttered up onto the sidewalk and tucked the three-wheeler into a loading dock of a neighboring clinic. He watched the street as if at any moment the militia bikers might appear.

"Try to relax," Miles said, but felt a twisting unease in his midsection. It wouldn't be long before word made it to Lieutenant Chati. They knew what Miles knew, and every minute counted.

Tristan was out of the wagon and began pacing. "What am I doing here?" he muttered.

"Go, if you have to. If you decide to stay, get ready to leave. I'm going in the church to ask about the man with the beard. If you see anyone come in behind me, send a text."

"All right. I can do that. I'll do that."

Miles didn't have time to calm Tristan down. Even the most advanced combat gear with auto-injecting ampules of performance drugs couldn't fully negate a good dose of adrenaline. Miles could only hope that Tristan wouldn't abandon him even as he felt a pang of guilt for having dragged the man this far. By now, the militia would have their faces, and Chati and friends could put the word out that their fellow officers had been attacked.

The inside of the church was cool and dark, with stackable chairs forming pews on either side of a broad aisle leading to a simple lectern on a dais. No cross, no symbol, just words in gold decorating the wall behind the speaker stand.

"Quench those who thirst. Feed those who hunger. Give relief to those who mourn."

Recorded guitar music played. Was it the same radio program from the soup kitchen?

A group sat in a circle on one side of the auditorium. A woman in a double-breasted low-collar coat rose to meet him. Her voice had the affected accent of a small habitat dweller, something he didn't hear often except from the oldest of returnees.

"I'm Pastor Hung. We have hours of worship posted on the information board. This is a private group."

"I'm not here to pray. I'm looking for this man."

Miles showed her the screen grab from the video with Agatha and the bearded man.

She barely glanced at it. "I'm afraid I can't help you."

"Take another look. It's important. Braided beard. Coat with a hood. He had this girl with him this afternoon. She's in danger."

After a second examination of the picture, Pastor Hung's jaw tightened. "I'll ask you to leave."

"Has anyone else come here looking? Cops, maybe? Because if they haven't, they will now."

"Many people come through these doors. We don't turn anyone away if they're peaceful. And as I said, we're in the middle of a private session."

"Do you know who the girl is? This is Agatha Fish. She's the daughter of Gennady and Beatrix. Between the two of them, they've got folks willing to hurt other people in their search for their girl."

"Just because you're the first bounty hunter here in this search means I should trust you?"

"I don't need you to trust me. I'm not after a reward. What I do need is her location, because she's the one in danger. Who is this man? He has her."

Pastor Hung glanced at the waiting group. "Si Lu, conduct the closing recital and prayer."

She led Miles to a back office. The spare room held little more than a desk and a set of chairs and a dusty miasma. She didn't sit after closing the door.

"You come in here with a weapon at your side and you want me to believe you're here out of concern for this girl?"

Miles had almost forgotten about the Yellow Tiger burner he had absconded with. He nudged the holster. "It's a long story. I just took it from someone who's willing to hurt people to find Agatha."

"And you're not?"

"I just want to bring her home."

"Even if that home is someplace where she's neglected and miserable?"

"So you know where she is. I'm no social worker. I don't pretend to understand what Agatha has gone through with her parents. But you people hiding her is bad enough. This is footage from a local pawn shop. The way she's clinging to this man—"

Pastor Hung sighed. "Henrik. His name is Henrik."

"And where is he?"

"He's one of our pastors. He would never hurt her. Agatha came here to help with our mission. Wanted to work with the community. Feed the hungry. She's a young girl who ran from home. I took her in and let her rest and hoped after a night away from her situation, she'd change her mind, because it's exactly what I did when she hid here for a day about a year ago. Then, she was okay to leave by evening. But this time she told me and Pastor Henrik who she was and what she had gone through. She was cutting herself, tried to kill herself twice in recent weeks with pills and whiskey. Me and Henrik and the other pastors discussed which hospital we should contact to assist when we learned about the search by the militia. Before we could reach a conclusion, Henrik took her."

"Why?"

"To keep her out of her parents' hands. Once we bring her to a hospital, they'll know, and her mother and father would have been contacted."

"When did Henrik take her?"

"A little after midnight. I had Agatha in a spare room in the women's dorm. Henrik had been outvoted in his suggestion to hide her here and bring a doctor to evaluate her and give her care. This morning we were going to drive her to the Wood Creek pediatric unit where I know someone who could talk to her."

The timing matched. From the church, Henrik must have been the one who went with Agatha to the mansion. So Pastor Henrik, Agatha, or both had then entered her home and stolen the ballerina and the other figurines.

"So you lost her," Miles said.

"We have staff looking for Henrik. Like I told you, he wouldn't hurt her. He'll return. This place is all he knows."

"Do you know that he took her to rob her own home."

"That...is troubling. But tell me, is it a robbery if the items belong to you?"

"Why?"

"It's like I said: Agatha wanted to help our mission. She wouldn't stop talking about it. Went on about how valuable her useless toys were, how many people she could help if she could sell them. She's an idealistic child."

"Who needs her parents, even if it's an unpleasant situation. So Henrik took her where?"

"Not to his apartment nor to any of our facilities." She sighed. "I was hoping he would answer his texts and return."

"We're past that. And the militia is coming at this hard enough that they won't hesitate to hurt this Henrik to get Agatha."

"There's one last location we haven't checked because it's not close. We have one of the old ruins in the desert. We used it before Seraph was anything more than a camp next to a clean water spring. We would hide dissidents and debtors fleeing from Meridian's long hand. Back then, the corporation would go to any lengths to capture someone it deemed troublesome or a rebel against their view of how Earth should be resettled. Most would continue their journey to the faction out at the ocean. But a few stayed here."

"I was alive for most of this. You don't look that old."

Pastor Hung only smiled placidly as she checked a device, then swiped the screen. "I've shared the location. Its old name is The Stone Where We Softened the Face of God. While Henrik shouldn't have acted without our consent, he did it to protect her. Promise me he won't be harmed."

Miles confirmed a ping on his map app some fifty kilometers out. "Why are you trusting me with this?"

"You're too old to be a Seraph cop, you're too rough-looking for a bounty hunter of the caliber the Fishes might hire, and my intuition tells me you actually want to bring Agatha home. Plus, the way those Yellow Tigers just pulled up outside of here, I'm guessing they're not with you."

She showed him her phone screen. He hadn't noticed security cameras, but the screen showed four different views of three desert runners with Yellow Tiger markings. Six cops piled out and headed for the church door, with Spikey Hair in the lead with a weapon in hand.

"There's a back way at the end of the hall," Hung said. "I'll set the alarm after you go through the door."

"What about you? They're angry, and you're going to want to stay out of their way."

She tucked her device into a pocket and straightened her collar. "I intend to welcome them."

Miles didn't want to delay another second to argue. He pushed the fanny bar to open the back door as Pastor Hung vanished into the church proper. Her voice and voices of the militia echoed. As Miles exited to the side of the building, a burner discharged from somewhere inside. He froze. Heard shouts. Screams. A second shot.

A cop appeared at the mouth of the alley. Red sideburns. He fumbled with his laser pistol. "He's out here!" Sideburns was momentarily distracted when something happened outside at the front of the church that caught his attention.

Someone screaming had just exited the building.

Miles ran for the corner at the back of the church. A flash. A tiny hole appeared in the wall next to him and sizzled as he made it to a rear lot. Sprinting past a rubbish bin, he heard boot steps clomping behind him. Up ahead, Tristan was waiting at the loading dock. But as Miles waved for him to start the vehicle, another desert runner pulled up. The driver sprang from the vehicle and pointed a burner at Tristan.

Tristan raised his hands and was quickly subdued.

The cop was too far away to charge on foot. The neighboring lot was mostly open space in bright sun. Miles turned back and made it to the corner just as Sideburns came charging after him. They collided and went down to the pavement. Sideburn's burner slid from his grip as Miles delivered a sharp blow to his throat.

He kneeled on Sideburn's chest. The cop with Tristan hadn't noticed. And the alley was still empty. Wouldn't be for long. Miles crushed the throat mike the cop was wearing and grabbed a set of keys from his waist.

As he rose, he took the trooper's burner. "You get up, I shoot you."

Miles hurried back down the side of the church. The emergency door squeaked as it opened. Men's voices. Miles put three shots into the door as he ran past, and three more when he made it to the street. Whatever militia troopers were inside weren't coming out. In front of the church, the members of Pastor Hung's group were scattering.

Miles tried to force himself to calm down, but Insight wasn't helping. He received a traffic update and weather report. A spec sheet on the desert runner obscured his view. Try as he might, he couldn't dismiss it. He dropped the cop's burner as he grappled with the key ring. One belonged to a vehicle. The doors on all the vehicles were swung up and open. He picked the middle one and jammed the key into the ignition.

If this wasn't the right one, he had just wasted more precious seconds. The cops would have backup. They'd come down the alley and out the front and he'd be dead.

The desert runner's engine purred to life. If the vehicle had an electronic lock or ID requirement, it hadn't been activated.

He backed up, slammed it in gear, and floored it. The church fell away behind him, but not before a group of militia appeared on the street. They had their weapons out, pointing at him, and Miles knew they'd follow him into the desert.

Chapter Twenty-Eight

With a sharp *thump,* the paved city street gave way to a dirt road.

Miles gripped the vibrating steering wheel and actively guided the vehicle over the rough ground. He almost dropped his phone as he pulled up the location Sister Hung had shared. It wouldn't synch with the runner's console screen.

Fifty-two klicks. The map app made no turns and displayed a thick pink line heading south for his route. Which meant it didn't know how to get him there and he'd have to pay close attention on the road ahead.

He was distracted as he examined the controls within the desert runner. The dashboard add-ons had a radio, a small computer, and a few modifications he didn't recognize. He could only hope none of them were a kill switch that could be triggered remotely.

A few kilometers down the dirt road, he came to his first split. Both lanes led roughly south, but the left one more so. The map app didn't recognize either. He veered left and kept his speed, racing into the bright evening.

A sign read Now Leaving Seraph.

Over the next thirty minutes, a group of five trucks passed him, heading towards the city. Otherwise, he saw no traffic. A second sign warned No Services Beyond This Point.

Miles exhaled and tried to focus. The militia had come into the church, guns blazing. He could only hope the cops hadn't shot anyone and would realize Tristan was only his ride and knew nothing. It didn't mean the cops wouldn't ask. He shuddered. And now the sign reminded him he was truly on his own, trusting that Sister Hung hadn't just provided a false lead to get rid of him.

"Miles Kim," a weary-sounding voice said from the radio. "This is Lieutenant Chati of the Yellow Tiger militia. You stole one of our patrol units and fired upon our officers. This is a last chance for you to turn around and surrender yourself. You'll be treated fairly and given due process. A good lawyer might even make sure you don't see more than a few weeks in lockup."

Miles hesitated for a moment before tapping the Talk button. "You'll get your car back. Your men came in hot and assaulted one of the soup kitchen managers."

"Some will say it was you who caused a commotion, assaulted an officer, and destroyed militia property. You opened fire with a burner."

"Let me talk to Captain Sin."

"This isn't a negotiation. You need to turn that vehicle around and surrender yourself. Otherwise, I can't help what's going to happen next. You'll be declared an outlaw and hunted down, not just by our militia, but by the other law enforcement agencies. You'll have the marshals and Red Banner troopers on your trail, and some aren't as restrained as my men."

"Why don't you want Agatha Fish to come home, Lieutenant?"

Chati was puffing hard into his microphone as if he were hyperventilating. "My people are handling this. You're interfering with an investigation you have no business in."

"I was hired by the girl's mother. Your cops got greedy. They're leading with their guns out and are only going to get her hurt."

"Last warning, Mr. Kim. Turn around now, or—"

Miles shut the radio off. Calmed his own breathing. Wiped sweat from his forehead. Focused on the dirt and gravel track ahead of him.

A second sign told him Rough Road Beyond This Point.

As if punctuating the sign's warning, he hit a rut and the desert runner bounced over a patch of broken hard earth where the road had partially washed out from some long-ago flash flood.

No services. Rough road. As if he had reached the corner of an old map of an unexplored world, racing towards a serpent-wrapped direction marker.

Abandon hope, because beyond this point, there be dragons.

***

He delayed turning on the headlights for as long as he dared but didn't want to bottom out the desert runner or get jammed on one of the big rocks jutting from the hardpan.

The road remained mostly visible, a faint track of smooth soil winding through the scrub. But trying to maintain any kind of speed meant on more than a few occasions missing a turn and plowing over rocks and brush and needing to guess which way the trail might be.

So far, the desert runner navigated each minor detour like a champ, albeit with bone and metal-jarring shudders that made his joints and brain ache. The kilometers peeled away, although the road was now veering too far south-westward.

Ten klicks to go.

He checked the rearview mirror for the umpteenth time. Saw no lights. Would the militia chance sending a flying drone out? The first responders to the train disaster had risked it during the day. And with Lieutenant Chati and his crew's reckless pursuit, nothing was off the table in their hunt to find Agatha before he did. If the Caretakers and Watchers above were still alive and had their eyes peeled, they wouldn't care who was violating their directive to stay out of the sky.

Someone would be punished.

Miles was itching to turn off the headlights to make it more difficult on anyone or anything in pursuit. Instead, he drove faster.

Nine klicks. Eight. Seven.

A long curve marked by boulders veered west. The waypoint on his app told him he needed to head southeast. Perhaps there was a turn ahead somewhere. In the dark, he couldn't tell whether the gray formations around him were rocks, hills, or clouds. His sense of distance was off. He slowed to roll down the window and had his eye mark what it could, as if searching for a target. Nothing besides the nearest crooked trees showed up on his display.

Following the road meant he could keep his speed, but the as-the-crow-flies waypoint would slip ever further away if he was wrong. And if Lieutenant Chati had likewise learned of Agatha's location, Miles would lose his precious lead.

Past the boulders, he found a narrow trail that crossed the sandy berm. He followed it, his foot tapping the accelerator. He was on a descending slope, which only grew steeper. The trail led to a series of switchbacks before leveling out, vanishing but then appearing again with stones as markers. He followed this for another six kilometers, crossing a dry streambed before once again climbing a long slope.

A low hill featured a flat plain, which appeared to have been graded. A row of old huts of mud and sheets of metal stood on one side where the track ascended through a stony pass. There were no lights and no signs of life. Miles climbed out and walked around the huts. They were little more than abandoned shanties. No one home, no belongings, no food wrappers or smells of cooking fires. The smoothed area held a few markers with rocks, as if someone had used it for a landing pad long ago. The crown of the hill above held the faintest glow. A fire, perhaps.

He got back in the runner. The cut in the rock threatened to scrape either side of his vehicle as he rolled slowly up the rutted path to the top of the ridge. It let out to a wide lot where a small electric car that had no business on rough roads sat parked.

A single structure dominated the top of the hill. It appeared to be a fort, a larger version of the temple but with an open roof. The headlights revealed separated or missing boards. Weeds grew everywhere, and banks of red-brown dust caked the exterior walls.

He killed the engine and turned off the lights. From beneath the passenger side dashboard, he unsnapped a flashlight. He checked the electric car first. Unlocked, but no keys. Battery compartment felt cool. It was dirty enough, but its tracks hadn't been eroded by weather. Someone had used it to drive to the abandoned fort recently.

"Henrik? Agatha?" he called.

His words were swallowed by the night. The wavering glow came from the fort's interior beyond a gateway where the doors had long since been knocked in and gone missing. He played the flashlight beam from side to side and up at the top of the wall. Parts of the roof had collapsed. If anyone was hiding up there, they were at risk of fall or injury. The whole place looked as if a solid wind might blow it down.

A campfire stood in the center of a courtyard strewn with rocks, disintegrating pieces of ancient machinery, a wagon, an old car of indeterminate model, and rubbish. A tarp tent stood against a far wall of a disintegrating blockhouse. The flickering flames caused the shadows to dance and move.

"I'm Miles Kim. I'm not a cop. I came here to find Agatha Fish. She's in danger."

A figure moved. Small. Fast. It darted from cover to cover and vanished near the tarp even as Insight tracked and targeted it.

Miles headed for the wall of the keep. "Agatha? Can you come out?"

A larger shape rose and came straight at him. The big man with the long beard squinted in the flashlight's beam and was holding an axe handle. Miles stopped and backpedaled as Henrik swung at him. Miles jumped out of the way, kicking up embers from the campfire as he scrambled to avoid another blow.

"Henrik! Valentino at the diner and Pastor Hung helped me get here to find you."

Henrik responded with a garbled cry. It sounded as if he had a sock stuffed into his mouth. He hopped across the campfire to cut Miles off. Was shaking the axe handle and raising it, all while muttering incomprehensively. The firelight illuminated a face full of scars and old skin grafts.

"Stop!" Agatha Fish cried. She had a hand up to Henrik as she appeared next to him. "Sister Hung told you to find us?"

Henrik's eyes remained fixed on Miles as if he was prepared to resume his assault at the girl's command.

Miles shined the light at them before lowering it to their feet. "Yeah, she did. There's a lot of people looking for you. Some aren't being nice about it, including the militia. I need to call Marshal Barma and get some help, get you someplace safe."

Henrik mumbled something which Miles didn't follow. Agatha responded, using sign language, and Henrik leaned his axe handle against his leg to make an emphatic reply likewise using hand gestures.

"He doesn't trust you," Agatha said. "Says you look like a police officer with your weapon."

"I used to be one. My name's Miles. Your mother hired me."

More sign language between the Agatha and Henrik. "More reason not to trust you, he says."

"You can't stay out here alone. I can't make either of you believe what I'm saying. There's no time for that. But you are in danger. This place is no longer a secret if I found you. I can call some people who will make sure you're not hurt. I know the marshal. He's a good man. Tell Henrik he can hang onto his weapon."

"He's not deaf."

When Miles pulled out his device to make the call, Henrik grabbed up the axe handle.

"Marshal Barma isn't part of the militia," Miles said. "He'll help with this situation."

The device had a signal. Weak, but just enough. Miles called. The phone rang.

Barma's gruff voice said, "What is it now?"

"It's Miles Kim. I have Agatha—"

The line beeped twice. He checked his phone. No signal. Had it faded or dropped out? He went out the gateway to the desert runner and clicked on the radio. Only snow. Henrik and Agatha followed, both watching him warily.

"You two need to hide."

"What's wrong?"

"Something's jamming radio communication. That means someone else is here, and they're close."

Chapter Twenty-Nine

Headlights cut white-blue swathes through the night as three vehicles climbed to the top of the lower hill. From Miles' vantage point at the upper ridge, he could target each vehicle, but doubted he would hit anything vital that would guarantee knocking them out.

He checked the charge on his burner. Six shots left. He cursed himself for dropping Sideburn's gun and for not recharging during the drive into the desert. He had counted six cops at the church, with another arresting Tristan. His estimate didn't include Lieutenant Chati and whatever additional militia he might bring with him if they were all coming.

And why wouldn't they? He was standing between them and whatever payday they would see by being the ones who found Agatha. He had opened fire on them. They would drop down on him like a metric ton of bricks.

The old fort, while it might have been defensible with enough firepower, was also a trap. The ridge closed around the old structure, with a sheer cliff on all sides. Anyone trying to climb down without light and equipment risked breaking their breadbasket. At least he knew they'd have to use the road.

The vehicles below stopped. It was too far to hear voices, but dark shapes climbed out of the lead car. Someone pointed his direction. Miles ducked.

Stupid. He had ignored the fact they might have infrared and night vision.

The militia vehicles' engines whined to life. They were coming up.

He slid down from his vantage point and made a quick check of his device. Still no signal. A military grade jammer would block any radio. He sprinted across the yard and hoped Agatha and Henrik had found a hole to hide in. If they stayed down, if they remained quiet...but no, he realized. They'd be found. Chati and Spikey Hair might be rotten apples in the militia, but this had evolved into an organized effort to take Agatha Fish. The cops coming up the slope would scour the fort, and from the appearance of the campsite, Henrik didn't appear to have planned much beyond their flight from Seraph.

"Agatha," he called. "Wherever you are, no matter what happens, stay down!"

He climbed the section of the wall, which had the remnants of a second floor. It was a narrow fit and he had to crouch. But it was an elevated position and suitable cover.

Keep the enemy bottled up. Keep them on the X. Don't stop shooting until they stop moving. Then shoot some more.

Good counsel for a platoon with a fully charged arsenal.

The words kept coming. Snippets. Memories. Images of military instructors. He blinked hard to clear his head. Realized while some of what he was recalling might have been real, the advice might also be misremembered or the product of his wife's serials.

The headlights wavered and played on the rocks by the trail.

Metal screeched from below. The lights stopped moving. He strained his ears. Thought he heard someone shout, then silence. Had they gotten hung up? Good, because it bought him moments. Bad, because now the Yellow Tigers would be on foot.

He surveyed the entry before the gateway. Bare dirt, mostly. At least they wouldn't have much cover until they crossed a stretch of open ground. With his Insight module, he could target the first ones out. Shooting them down would make the rest hold back. He didn't want to ponder the possibility of a siege. Already his knees ached. Keeping this position for much longer would mean his legs would fall asleep.

The soft electric whir came at him from above. Drone. The dark object wasn't much bigger than his hat. It hovered before he zeroed in on it and nailed it with a shot from his burner. The thing popped and fell like a stone.

Five shots left, and now they undoubtedly knew his location. He dropped from his perch. Found an opening at the wall. His view was partially obstructed by dead vegetation, but at least it would take the incoming goons an extra fraction of a second to find him. He leaned out and sighted down the top of his weapon. Breathed.

"Miles Kim, we know you're in there," Spikey Hair's amplified voice called. "You come out now, we arrest you. No one gets hurt. The girl goes home."

Miles tried to blink dust out of his left eye.

"This all can end peacefully."

The burner felt heavy, even though he was holding it in his artificial hand.

"We all come out ahead if you surrender."

Every drop of moisture had left his mouth.

These militia troopers were willing to hurt people to get Agatha. They had come guns blazing at the Church of the Sands. Miles didn't want to shoot a cop doing his duty, but these clowns weren't serving Seraph. He felt certain they needed Agatha alive, whether it was for money, leverage against the Fishes, or both. His one advantage? With her present, the incoming thugs might not use heavy weapons.

An object came sailing through the air into the center of the courtyard. A grenade, Insight identified helpfully.

Miles hugged the wall as a starburst flared and a thunderous *WHUMP* shook the ground and shattered the air. They'd be coming on the tail of the flashbang. But despite having ducked, his good eye was half blind with after-images of the explosion and his artificial eye was struggling to compensate. His ears rang. He'd have to trust his Insight module.

Ignoring the bright phantoms burned into his vision, he leaned out again, weapon up, and just in time. Three armored figures came charging towards the campfire. Embers which had been scattered by the blast burned orange. The in-coming militia troopers were carrying rifles and swept the air before them, one heading straight for Miles.

Miles shot him first and squeezed off a couple more shots at the other two before a section of wall erupted in dust and smoke. Miles dove to the ground as the barrage of automatic return fire peppered the air, the fort, and the sur-rounding dirt.

Insight still had a target locked. Miles raised his burner to fire again blindly, hoping the link between his brain, eye, and hand would do the heavy lifting. A brilliant crackle and a deep pop assaulted his ears as something flashed ahead of him. His cybernetic eye went blank, and with it, his Insight module and his target.

The armored man strode through the settling dust, his shoulder spotlights sweeping the ground until they found Miles.

"Ha!" Spikey Hair called. "Didn't think we'd need these old munitions. But the captain was right for once, telling us to keep them stocked in the cars just in case."

Miles' heart sank. An electric pulse round would deactivate drones and scramble cybernetics. Waves of agony rolled through Miles' brain, making his temples throb and every nerve from his neck down to his crotch ache. Phantom pain or real, he could barely keep his eyes open and struggled not to curl into a ball and whimper.

Spikey Hair had a stubby shotgun leaning on his shoulder. He kicked Miles over onto his back and punted the burner aside.

"You have any idea how much she's worth? We could have cut you in, if you hadn't been such a mossback. But this gets pretty easy to wrap up here and now, you having shot at us."

From behind him, Sideburns said, "Hey, Mikey, Cutty needs a medic."

"Just a sec. Let's wrap up our business with Mr. Kim."

"Just shoot him and get it done. We still have to find the girl."

"Relax, Pim. She isn't going anywhere. Mr. Kim needs to tell us who else he has looped in on his little bounty hunt so we get no more surprises—"

Spikey Hair screamed as Henrik launched himself at him, roaring and striking the armored man with a wild haymaker that knocked Spikey Hair into the dirt and sent his weapon tumbling. Sideburns fired. A three-round burst dropped Henrik. Miles grabbed a cricket ball-sized rock, rose, and threw it left-handed, nailing Sideburns. He then dove for Spikey Hair's dropped shotgun. He discharged the weapon, squeezing the trigger over and over until the shotgun went dry.

Too much dust to see anything. But three men were groaning. Henrik lay next to him, unconscious or dead. The distinct aroma of burned skin lingered.

Miles' ears echoed from the shotgun blasts, and a high-pitched ringing lingered from the grenade. His right arm remained sluggish and uncooperative as he fought to stand.

Insight, wake up.

But his module ignored him. His right eye remained blank, and the jabs of pain running down his body made him grit his teeth. He patted Spikey Hair down, pulling a burner from a hip holster. He discarded the spent shotgun. The young cops had just been reminded that electric rounds still packed a palmful of steel pellets and could hurt flesh and blood besides screwing up cybernetics.

Muffled radio chatter warbled from the helmets.

Miles likewise disarmed the other two men, but the first he had shot was no longer moaning. Miles pulled the helmet off. Weak pulse. One of the burner rounds had found a gap between the chest piece and the shoulder guard.

He took the man's throat mike. "This is Miles Kim. Three of your men need medical attention. Send one cop up if you want to help them."

An uncertain trooper responded, her shaky voice crisp from the militia man's helmet. "Put Mikey on."

"Mikey's not going to be talking to anyone if you don't hurry. And if we see one weapon or another drone, they get executed."

Spikey Hair glared at him. He had flecks of blood oozing from lacerations on his face. Sideburns had his head back and his eyes closed as he gritted his teeth.

"On second thought, make it two cops with their med kits and a stretcher. You'd better hurry."

Miles had time to ponder why Lieutenant Chati wasn't the one talking to him. The most obvious reason was that he wasn't on scene. He had sent his team of grunts to collect Agatha. Miles fought through waves of nausea as he fought to stay upright. He eyed the dark ridgeline.

One spry goon with a rifle, and it would be over, he thought numbly.

When the militia finally showed, it was two troopers, one man, one woman, both with helmet and armor. The man was actually waving a handkerchief about.

Miles had returned to his position at the base of the wall and kept the burner trained. "Your friends are there. Keep things slow and steady and tell me if you're going to do anything that needs you to power something up."

They tended to the first of the wounded. After stripping the young man out of his armor, they gelled the wounds and shot him up with drugs. They popped out a stretcher and carried him away.

Spikey Hair gasped and was panting. "What do you think you're accomplishing here? You don't get to walk away from this."

"You're probably right."

"When our backup arrives, you're dead."

The two cops returned to assist Sideburns onto another stretcher.

"We'll see. You should save your strength and shut up before I decide I want a hostage."

The threat worked. He shut up. When the cops returned for Spikey Hair, Miles pointed to Henrik. "Check him first."

They kneeled next to the bearded man without comment, opening his shirt and examining him. The burner wounds weren't bleeding, but all three had struck his chest.

The female trooper said, "He's alive. He needs a doctor and a hospital."

"And I'm guessing he gets neither unless you get the girl."

She eyed him warily through the face shield of her helmet. "You want us to take him or not?"

"No!"

It was Agatha. She ran from the shadows and dropped next to Henrik. Tears streamed from her eyes as she sobbed. The two cops looked at each other. A long second passed as if they were considering grabbing her or going for a concealed weapon, of which Miles felt reasonably certain they both had tucked away somewhere with their gear.

"Get back, Agatha," Miles said. "Henrik is hurt. These two sworn officers of the law are going to help him and get him to a doctor. Aren't you?"

The female cop nodded. With effort they loaded Henrik onto the stretcher and carried him off. Miles walked to Agatha and led her away from Spikey Hair, who watched Miles with unrestrained rage in his eyes.

"You're going to be okay," Miles said. "Henrik will be okay. But you need to go hide again, and not come out unless I come find you."

"What's the point?" Spikey Hair asked. "You get killed and we get her. You give her up? We get her and you get to live."

Miles watched until Agatha vanished again into the gloom of the fort. "I won't use a child as a bargaining chip."

But those words nagged at Miles even as Spikey Hair was taken by his returning comrades.

Miles would die. There was no way around it. If they were willing to use drones, they'd send another in with a frag grenade, and it would all be over. He knew he should move. But his head was full of fuzz, and the ringing reached a new crescendo. He leaned against the wall of the fort. Guessed if he tried to find a new defensive position, he might collapse, and he meant to make Lieutenant Chati's second wave of attackers pay if they wanted to take Agatha.

The sky turned shades of brighter gray as he waited. Insight rebooted. His right eye could see again. The more he thought about it, stepping out the fort's gate to face the militia would spare Agatha from a chance stray round or whatever heavier ordinance the militia might dust off and bring to bear to take down the old cyborg standing in their way.

Miles checked the burner charge for the umpteenth time. His stomach grumbled, and he would have traded his hat for a swallow of water. Tried to stay in the moment, focused, but couldn't shake the heaviness of his limbs.

He made it to the gateway and waited.

***

A lone militia goon appeared, walking into the outer lot with purpose. She was unarmored, sporting the Yellow Tiger tunic buttoned up to her neck. A monocle was fixed to her eye.

Captain Santabutra Sin paused to show her palms. "Kim?" she called. "I'm unarmed."

"Stop there."

"I've got four wounded men heading towards Wood Creek Hospital in Seraph. Care to tell me what's going on?"

"Figured you would have been briefed. And I'm surprised to see you here."

"Can you come closer? I don't like to scream this early in the morning. And Lord knows I've done enough of it already."

Miles kept the burner at his side as he emerged from cover. His legs tingled and he felt cramps looming. "Your sniper have a clean shot now?"

"There's no sniper. I'm too senior to be on the front line of an op like that."

"Figured Lieutenant Chati would send in the troops."

"He probably would, if he were here. But he's not. You were lucky the lance that got here first had a disagreement whether to launch an assault. Now I have ten troopers down that road who can resolve this."

"You're not taking the girl."

"Let me see her so I know she's alive."

Miles studied the captain's face. Despite the freckles, she appeared older than he had first guessed, with etched creases on her eyes and mouth and dark circles a testament to a lack of recent sleep.

Captain Sin sighed. "Look, Kim, I promise you she won't be hurt. Neither will you, assuming you do nothing stupid. This whole thing has spun out of control. I've got six troopers locked up in my patrol wagon and three more shot up, thanks to you. My boss is going to make heads roll for this, including mine. Lieutenant Chati learned about a reward for the girl being offered by a third party. He hasn't come clean with everything yet, but it was a fat enough wad of credits that even I considered it for a hot second. But Agatha has been through enough. It's time for her to go home."

"Go home where?"

"Fair question. I checked the court order. Home with her mother. Where she belongs."

Chapter Thirty

Miles holstered his burner as he picked his way through the fort's interior. A massive beam lay canted between two failing walls. Miles winced as he brushed it while scooching beneath. Trickles of dust waterfalled down around him. Didn't collapse. He made it to the opposite side before calling out, "Agatha, it's Miles."

It was the fourth time he had called for her. Captain Sin had promised to remain in the courtyard and was now out of sight behind him. Miles peered beneath a leaning sheet of rotting wood before moving on to check a collapsed side room.

"Agatha?"

She emerged from a covered hole in the floor at the end of the corridor. In the dawn's light, her face was a mask of dirt and dried tears.

He dropped to a knee. "The lady outside will take you home."

"I don't want to go home. I want to stay here."

"I understand that. When you're older, you get to make that decision, but not now. Henrik isn't your father. You can't be out here alone. The court says you're supposed to live with your mother. When you're eighteen, you can decide to go wherever you want. And that time will come faster than you can imagine. Then you get to figure out which one of your parents you want in your life."

"I don't want to be with my mother. I don't want to be with my father."

"If we got everything we wanted, life would get pretty boring."

She raised an eyebrow and gave Miles an are-you-serious look.

"Agatha, tell me what you *do* want."

"I want to help the people who are hungry down at the kitchen."

"You learned about them on the radio program, didn't you?"

She nodded.

"How did you get to know Henrik?"

"Celia took me there and let me deliver a trunk load of groceries. She took me again a few more times whenever she had errands. I sorted food donations in the back for an hour each time we went. Henrik worked the stockroom alone most of the time. He didn't enjoy being up front serving or with the kitchen staff because of how he looked."

"Did you feel sorry for him?"

"No. But I knew he was sad. No one at the kitchen could understand him because of his throat and mouth. I tried. And then I found out he spoke sign language."

"He taught you sign language?"

"Uh-uh. I taught myself. It took a month. The next time Celia brought me by, we had our first conversation. The time after, he told me what happened to him in a fire when he was home alone when he was a little boy. Is he okay?"

"The medics are helping him. He's fine." Miles tried to control his voice. "Agatha, I have to ask you a question, and it's important. Has Henrik ever touched you in a way that made you feel uncomfortable?"

"You mean sex abuse? Eww, no. I don't like him like that. Celia insisted on being with me every time we were at the kitchen. Nothing happened."

"Okay. When we go back, you know you'll have to tell this story. Tell it like you told me. Believe it or not, your mother misses you. She threw a party for you, but you weren't there. She got you a horse. A real one."

"I don't like horses."

"Maybe your mom should know that. There's a bunch of things your mom needs to know about. But like I said, she's your mother. And it's time we go see her."

**

Captain Sin was speaking on her com when Miles brought Agatha out of the fort. She switched the com off as they approached. Stooped to look at Agatha.

"So you're the little girl who came all this way into the desert."

Agatha clutched Miles' hand and didn't respond. They walked together down the rocky slope where one of the militia tanks, a pair of electric motorbikes, and a few runners waited, along with some nervous-looking militia.

Captain Sin put her hand out to Miles. "Your burner? It will make everyone less itchy for the ride back."

"Not on your life. I ride with Agatha."

The captain dropped the topic and went to the tank and climbed into the back. Miles helped Agatha up and they joined her. The climate control churned out cool air. The morning outside promised to be a hot one.

A militia cop with a medic badge on his shoulder joined them. The boy had more pimples than chin hairs. "Are either of you injured? I'd like to examine you."

"Go ahead," Miles said. "No shots."

The checkup was brief, the medic checking Agatha's eyes, skin, arms, and legs, with a temperature check with a scanner preceding the diagnosis. "You're a healthy young girl."

He raised the scanner to Miles.

"I'm fine. You're done. Ride in a different car."

The medic climbed out and closed the door. The driver started the tank up, and the procession began its trip across the broken track of desert towards Seraph.

"You arrested my driver," Miles said.

"He's in holding for questioning at the station after the shootout at the church. He's okay."

"Was anyone hurt? Pastor Hung—"

"Shaken. No civilians were harmed. None of my officers, either."

"I want Tristan released."

"It's not that simple for him or you."

"Is that where you're taking us? The station?"

"Considering everything, yes," she said. "You'll have to hand over the pistol when we get there, you know."

"We go by her mother's first. Agatha goes home, then I'm all yours."

"Were you always this difficult when you were with Meridian, Kim?"

He put on his winningest smile. "As a matter of fact, yes. And you can call me Miles."

Chapter Thirty-One

Miles breathed faster as the armored vehicle rumbled down the road between the fancy mansions leading to Beatrix Fish's home. He had fought to avoid dozing off during the ride, anticipating at any moment that they would be ambushed or Captain Sin would try some last-minute ploy, either drugging him, shooting him, or drugging him then shooting him. But once they got to the relatively smooth city roads, she had stayed busy on a tablet, texting furiously the whole time. Now the sleepies were gone, replaced by an antsiness as if he had just been jabbed with a stim injection.

Agatha, meanwhile, stared blankly out the window at the scenery and resolutely straight ahead once they entered Seraph.

Beatrix, Kitty, Celia, and three of the maids stood waiting by the entry. The tank threw up a cloud of dust as it lurched to a stop.

"I need to talk to Beatrix Fish first," Miles said.

Captain Sin's eyes narrowed. "Should I be worried?"

"If anyone starts shooting, it won't be me. Agatha, can you wait here?"

The girl nodded. Miles climbed out of the vehicle. Beatrix moved towards the tank, but Miles stopped her.

"Get out of my way," Beatrix said. "Where's my daughter?"

"She's in there. I thought we should chat first."

"Chat? What are you talking about? Let me see her."

"I know that's what you want. I need to believe you mean it. Agatha's a special girl who needs a lot of attention."

"I give her attention."

"Don't interrupt me. I want to make sure you really want her. I need to know she won't just be an ornament to be dangled in front of your friends or a game piece you taunt your ex with."

"How dare you."

"I dare like this. There must be a reason the court awarded you custody, but from what I've seen, I can't figure out why. She may as well be back with Gennady if she's going to be shut up in a room and ignored. She needs help, real help, and while she's young, she needs to be respected and listened to and given guidance, and you need to act like a mother and treat her like a daughter."

Mrs. Fish's face had reached a state of red. "You have no right to talk to me like this."

"I don't, except the parts where you know I'm right. What I'm asking is for you to talk to Agatha. Include Celia on the conversation. There's a reason Agatha ran away. Find out what she wants and who she is. It might surprise you."

"All right, Mr. Kim, you had your say," she said flatly. "You'll have your credits, if that's what this is about. Don't think you're the first man who's tried to use my wealth and status as a bludgeon against me."

"It's not about you or me. It's about her. She shouldn't have left home like this. But you need to understand what led up to it so it doesn't happen again. I didn't take this job to make friends or to find a whale client to tap during my stay in Seraph. I told you I'd bring your daughter home. I did. This conversation is about giving you the chance to make it so she never *wants* to leave."

"If you're done, step out of my way."

Miles did. Agatha popped open the door and slid down out of the vehicle. She and her mother embraced. Agatha remained stiff as her mother cried and promised and made a show of it. Maybe some of it was real. Beatrix took Agatha to the line of servants, and they all conducted the young girl with them inside.

Kitty smirked through it all. "In she goes. My mother's favorite tchotchke, ready to be dangled from the chandeliers and Christmas tree branches for all to adore. I'm sure there's time to plan another gala for next Friday night. Care to make a wager?"

"I'm a little light. Are you happy Agatha's home?"

"It'll be good to have things calmer around here. My mother breaks out in her stress rashes so easily. I'll never hear the end of her moaning, and Celia's hands will reek of ointment for days."

"You let Agatha in last night, didn't you?"

The smirk faltered. "Excuse me?"

"You sound like your mother when you say that. You heard me."

"What are you accusing me of?"

"Turning off the alarm. That's how she got in. All the guests and day staff had left. It wasn't an intruder like your mother suspects. And I don't think your sister knows how to do that. She's bright, but she doesn't even have a set of house keys."

"Surely Celia forgot to set the alarm."

"She didn't. I reviewed the logs. And somehow you turned it off without the system recording the event. Or the history was altered. Something a programmer and whiz like you might manage."

Kitty was frowning. A storm brewed behind her eyes. "And what do you believe you know?"

"Me? Not much, ever, except that you're a bored girl who stirs up trouble. You could have told your mother Agatha was here, done something, I don't know. Maybe you figured out what your sister was planning. Perhaps she confided in her older sister, and you gave her a push in the wrong direction. This could have gone worse than it did."

"And that's what you're going to go to my mother with? Your intuition that I've been bad?"

"I was hired to bring Agatha home. I'm finished here."

"Hmm. You were hired, weren't you? And like any mercenary, you expect you'll be paid. I wonder if my mom will allow the transaction?" She leaned close. Her hair smelled sweet, honey or coconut. Maybe both. "I can make sure she pays. She tracks none of the expenses. We could even see your rate doubled. Or, just the same, maybe she'll forget, and this will be a giant waste of your time and energy. All you'll be left with will be your laundry bill, assuming all this soil will ever come off. I imagine a few credits in your account might mean we get to find some other task for you—hey!"

Miles was done. He marched back to the armored car and climbed in.

Captain Sin had a foot up on the seat and was resting her head on her knee. "All finished? That looked unpleasant."

"I was hoping you'd formally arrest me so we could leave."

"There's time for that. Am I adding loitering charges to my mental notes, or harassing the gentry?"

"If this was anyplace but Seraph, I'd know you were joking."

It was the first smile he got from her. "You haven't known me for long. I don't joke. Time to go downtown."

Chapter Thirty-Two

Marshal Barma was the largest person in the room. He paced back and forth between the empty desks, his hard leather boots creaking and clomping. His long duster hung open, revealing his ample gut and large hand cannon dangling from his shoulder. He was absently holding his hat and tapping it on his hand.

Captain Sin appeared content to watch him. Her monocle was on, and she had her tablet displaying a virtual screen only she could easily read. The data and images reflected in the glass of her eye piece. Miles might have used Insight to make it out, but decided not to rock the boat further as he sat opposite her at her desk. The rest of the office was empty, but voices could be heard just outside.

"Yellow Tiger enforcement ends at the city limits," Barma said. It wasn't a question. Neither Captain Sin nor Miles replied. The marshal made another lap up and down the office. "Principle of hot pursuit applies, but your officers who were pursuing had just terrorized a church group having a meeting. They discharged their weapons and just missed the pastor. Your lance officer also punched an employee at the Church of the Sands charity kitchen."

"Neither the kitchen assistant manager nor Pastor Hung want to press charges," Captain Sin said.

"Mayor Bedford doesn't care. He wants to see the troopers involved prosecuted."

"They're all in holding."

"You mentioned that. But then we come to Miles Kim. Shot a burner through the window of the soup kitchen, destroyed militia property, fired at militia troopers at the church, and finally shooting up the cops who came to the ruins of this fort to rescue Agatha Fish."

"Kidnap, not rescue," Miles offered.

"Huh. Jury's still out on that. While I've heard no one suggest Mr. Kim was an associate of this Henrik, they were cooperating in stopping your Yellow Tigers from acquiring the girl and willing to use deadly force. Miles says he was no longer in service of Beatrix Fish."

"I'm right here. And I wasn't."

Barma went on as if Miles hadn't spoken. "The sheriff should do this. But you know how her office gets."

Miles didn't know. But he didn't want to derail Barma's train of thought now going full speed.

"Mr. Kim consistently acted to find Agatha. He called me when he made it to the fort. I've heard nothing to suggest he was going to take her and try to extort money for her return. Same goes for this Henrik. Your troopers who assaulted him all had issues with their cameras but forgot to switch off one of their vehicles' microphones. Thanks for sharing that, Captain. It doesn't sound like Mr. Kim had much of a choice but to defend himself and the girl, considering what happened here in Seraph. I'm assigning no criminality to his actions. Agatha is home. As far as my office and what we're telling the mayor, this incident is a wrap, and the sheriff will have to decide whether any crime was committed inside Seraph that needs to be investigated."

Barma eyed both the captain and Miles before letting out a sigh, as if his deliberation had taken a toll, or he had just hiked out to the desert fort and back on foot. He still had bruises on his face from the events following the attack on the train, and his left wrist and hand were set in a cast.

Captain Sin dismissed the screens and adjusted the monocle. "As far as my command is concerned, my recommendation to my superiors is to punish the troopers involved and see they don't work in any capacity of law enforcement within Seraph."

"Is that what happens?" Miles asked. "They just get fired? Is Lieutenant Chati on the hook? He was spearheading the hunt for Agatha. Check your radio logs."

"I'm looking into his role in this," she said sharply. "The mayor and sheriff will no doubt hash it out. But I wouldn't hold your breath. Something like this goes to trial, it exposes the Fishes to a lot of media they don't want."

"Hate for them to get embarrassed."

"It's how things work here. I'm sure it's not so different with Meridian if a couple of members of her board of directors got exposed in a scandal. It means you're a free man once the sheriff approves the marshal's recommendation. You should look happy."

"That is his happy face," Barma said.

Miles clenched his jaw. "None of your troopers would have come at me like they did if the Fishes hadn't offered a bounty for Agatha."

"Not a crime to put out a reward."

"A reward for information is one thing. I'll bet you ask those troopers of yours, you'll find they had incentive to make sure Agatha was handed back to whichever parent was putting up the most cash, perhaps even hoping for a bidding war."

"Anything else?" Captain Sin asked.

"Yeah. Tristan, my driver?"

"Is waiting outside the front gate. Now if you excuse me, I have paperwork to file."

***

Miles and Barma walked down the corridor out into the courtyard. The militia staff on hand gave them sidelong glances but otherwise steered clear. The late morning sun was up and over the walls of the compound and was already making the concrete hot enough to cook a full breakfast.

"Buy you tea?" Miles offered.

"I'm going back to the office, bark at Glenda so she feels loved, and cover my ass with a flowery report of yesterday's events."

"Good. Because I'm broke."

Barma flapped his duster as if to dispel the heat. "Beatrix Fish didn't pay out?"

"Not yet."

"Don't hold your breath. You don't get that much money by squaring up with your contractors. And I'm guessing your arrangement wasn't in writing."

"I'm just worried about Agatha."

"I'm sure Beatrix Fish will contact you for parenting tips."

"My son works with doctors and therapists. I want to have one of them that isn't Dr. Varner see Agatha. Can you include that in your recommendations?"

"It won't help. There's no requirement for either Mr. or Mrs. Fish to follow through with anything we recommend. They committed no crime, from what I can tell. There's no leverage."

"Yeah, because that's all that matters, right?"

"Send me the rec. I'll include it. I'll forward it to the mayor, but he's head deep between Gennady's cheeks, so I doubt it will get traction."

A guard buzzed open the pedestrian gate leading outside the walls. Miles had to lower his hat to keep the bright daylight out of his eyes.

Tristan crouched on his heels nearby, resting in the shadow of the armored vehicle blocking half the sidewalk. He watched Miles and Barma warily.

Barma nodded a goodbye before squeezing into a subcompact hatchback parked across the street and sped off.

"We're done?" Tristan asked.

"Loose ends. Always loose ends."

"They say I can pick up my ride from impound. But there's a fee."

"I'll take care of it."

"You have credits?"

"No. Let's see about your tuk-tuk and we'll go from there."

***

A text message to Captain Sin and an hour later, and Tristan had his vehicle. During that time, Miles contacted the doctor Dillan had recommended and gave her a general summation of Agatha's situation. The doctor couldn't promise anything, but she offered to do what she could, assuming Miles could arrange a meetup. The unspoken bugbear was parental permission.

Tristan was filling out a release form on a tablet when Miles called Celia.

"Can you talk?" he asked.

"Yes. Mrs. Fish is with her masseuse, and the session always lasts ninety minutes."

"I'm forwarding a contact to you. She's a doctor who has experience with children who've experienced abuse. She can help Agatha if you can take her there."

"Things are difficult here. Agatha isn't allowed to leave the house with me after it was revealed I took her to the charity kitchen to work. I made the case to Mrs. Fish that it means a great deal to Agatha."

"Bold. What did she say?"

"Mrs. Fish was upset. She said she would see. It is as close to a change of mind as I have ever heard from her."

"You're amazing. And the fact that you're still employed means there's a chance Mrs. Fish will listen to you. It's the only thing we can do. Otherwise, I'm guessing Agatha is going to bolt again, and this time she might wind up in worse hands than Henrik. Suggesting Beatrix accompany her daughter would be too much to ask."

"I hear in your voice that you care, Mr. Kim."

"It's Miles. And I'm finishing what I started."

"Despite being fired."

"Yes. We save the ones we can. Sometimes the number is no greater than one."

There was rustling on the line, as if Celia had placed her device down. He heard muffled conversation before Celia said, "Excuse me. Kitty requires my assistance and I have to go. But before I do, I wish to send you something."

His phone dinged. A credit deposit required his thumbprint to accept. The credit service account showed the payment was from Celia Contreras.

"What's this for?" he asked.

"It is a thank you gift. Agatha is dear to me. And while it is but a token of what Mrs. Fish owes you, you've earned your wage, and it is only proper you receive a measure of compensation."

Miles couldn't think of anything to say but "Thank you."

Celia ended the call.

Tristan was finished with the release form and waiting nearby. "You have credits?"

Miles did. He loaded a chip and handed it to Tristan. "Not a fortune, and not what was promised, but it'll keep your wife from locking you out of the house."

Chapter Thirty-Three

Miles sat across from Dillan beneath the shade of an outdoor dining area. A terra cotta fountain on the wall trickled water. A sprig of miniscule white flowers sat in a thin shot glass center table. The late lunch crowd chatted away nearby, with the casually dressed diners picking at tapas and humus platters.

A server dropped off their food: soy crab cakes for Dillan and a portobello and ricotta flatbread for Miles. Both had mint tea on ice before them, the glass mugs heavy with condensation.

The server placed a hand on Dillan's shoulder. "Will there be anything else?"

"This looks perfect," Dillan said.

Once she left, Miles said, "She likes you."

"Not everyone who's friendly is flirting, Dad."

"If I had ignored the signs, you wouldn't be here."

"Fair enough. But you know I have a girlfriend. You sure you can afford this?"

"I haven't received the bill yet. If there're no prices on the menu, it's free, right?"

"I was seven when I said that," Dillan said. "I hate to rush, but I have twenty minutes before I need to get back to work."

"Then dig in."

The mushrooms on Miles' plate were earthy and full of umami and sprinkled with tasty oil. The flatbread was soggy. He washed it down with the tea, which had been overly sweetened. But he gestured to the server for a refill.

"You said you were working?" Dillan asked through a mouthful of food.

"A case with a young girl who ran away from her mother's home. Her parents used her to get back at each other. And when she got away from her father, they both sent people to find her. I was offered a lot of money, but some of the hunters got greedy."

"Did anyone get hurt?"

"Yes. But the girl made it back home to her mother."

"Because of you."

"Yes."

"And you're worried about the prices here?"

Miles washed down the last of his flatbread with a gulp of tea. "I didn't get paid. The mother wanted things done her way. Her way might have hurt the girl."

"And that's something you would never let happen. So how much was she worth?"

"Can't say. Enough that it got a unit of militia to come after her hard, along with anyone with her. I talked to the doctor you recommended. Shared the name with the girl's caretaker."

"Hopefully it will do some good. But you look worried."

"It's just me thinking."

"While you're doing that, I have a show tomorrow night. I want to give you a couple of tickets."

"How late is it? I get cranky after sundown."

"It's not that late. Will you come?"

"I only need one ticket."

"Each has a plus-one involved. Come alone, if you want, but come."

"I will."

Dillan dabbed his mouth with the cloth napkin and got up. The server smiled at Dillan and watched him leave before stopping at the table.

"Was everything to your satisfaction?" she asked.

"Yeah. Bring me the check. And another refill of tea while you're at it."

***

Captain Santabutra Sin answered after the first ring. "What is it, Kim?"

"No emergency. I was just checking to see if you have anything going on tomorrow evening?"

"I never answer a question like that without more information."

"Words of wisdom. My son has a musical performance. I can't guarantee it's anything you or I will even like. But I have tickets."

"You're asking me on a date? You're an involved party in a live investigation. If the mayor or sheriff office decide against Barma's recommendations, you're going to be facing charges."

"I'm on pins and needles in anticipation of the outcome. This isn't a date. I have an extra seat. I don't know anyone else in town, and it was either you or the marshal. I called you first."

"Is there food involved in this non-date?"

"Unless militia captains don't eat," Miles said.

"They eat. I'm just not up for being grilled any more on the Fishes, their daughter, or how the Yellow Tigers are handling the internal investigation."

"I consider myself forbidden from broaching any of these subjects."

"I'm a private person. My evenings are my quiet time. My every instinct is to say no."

"You can eat and dash. I won't be offended. I have no expectations except that my son is going to be playing music, the crowd will probably be younger than anything I'll feel comfortable in, and I'll be grateful to have someone at my table so I don't stick out like a sore thumb. I can pretend to be your chaperone and you were stood up on a date, if that makes the evening more fun."

"You're not selling this," Captain Sin said. "We'll both be sore thumbs."

"That's still not a no."

"I see nothing good out of saying yes. But I am curious. What time?"

"Meet me at seven. I'll send you the address. And thank you. Seraph is new grounds for me. It took me decades to decipher Meridian territory and River City, and I barely scratched the surface before retirement. This is your hometown and a whole new onion to peel."

"Will there be this many metaphors tomorrow evening?"

"The well is empty. I'll see you tomorrow."

Thanks for reading *The Atomic Ballerina*. I hope you enjoyed the story!

Miles Kim's adventure continues in *A Haunt of Jackals*, available March 1st, 2022.

His first case as a Seraph marshal may be his last.

When Seraph's head marshal calls in Miles Kim to help investigate a triple murder, Miles finds three bodies with no simple answers.

Why were a water baron, a militia leader, and an information broker meeting in a remote junkyard away from their bodyguards?

With no witnesses and no survivors, the case will thrust Miles into the center of a power struggle between the militia and Seraph's underworld. And no one wants an ex-Meridian police officer prying into their business.

Learning the truth will put Miles in the crosshairs of Seraph's sheriff and the local militia, along with a gang of ruthless cybernetic assassins on the trail of anyone getting close to the answers to what happened that night.

It will take all his skills as an investigator and all his wits to stop a series of events which will shake Seraph to its foundation.

Keep reading for a preview.

A Haunt of Jackals

Miles drove Tristan's three-wheeler through the dark streets past the cargo containers, which made up the bulk of the shanty town on the west side of Seraph. Insight labeled the neighborhood Bright Blocks, as if the cheery name could obscure the fact that a good portion of the district's residents lived in squalor. The weak headlights barely illuminated the uneven road.

He navigated down the ever-narrowing lanes until crossing a flood protection berm. The cargo containers gave way to the Seraph dump, a sprawling landfill with several scrapyards operated amid a trash-strewn stretch of wasteland. While fences marked several properties, most of the wide space was nothing more than competing heaps of refuse. Hulks of abandoned vehicles lined the side of the road. Drums with unknown contents lay partially buried. Dark stretches of dirt glistened as unknown liquids congealed on the ground.

Even the most desperate among Seraph's residents avoided living here. Warning signs hung askew on posts and the remnants of rusty galvanized steel barriers.

Keep Out. Danger. Hazardous Material.

An acrid stench stung Miles' nose. Tristan's wagon had no side windows or doors.

Miles slowed to a crawl and checked his device. Took a turn past a tall mountain of broken furniture and printed household goods. Stacks of cargo crates large enough to house small vehicles lined the way. The ground grew muddy. Miles didn't dare drive any faster lest the vehicle got bogged down.

The location Marshal Barma had pinged was close. What could possibly be out here? The rational question yielded to the facts of Miles' own experience as a cop. Bad things happened in remote locations.

A subcompact electric vehicle stood parked by a collection of massive containers. The containers stood open and dark. Miles parked a few paces away and left the headlights shining as he killed the engine and got out.

Barma's imposing form appeared at the threshold of the largest container. "Turn off those lights."

Miles did.

The marshal switched on a flashlight to illuminate the ground. "Took your time coming."

"Early morning traffic. Please don't tell me you called me here to remind me I don't know my way around town."

"This way. And mind your step. The floor gets sticky."

The cargo container's interior was damp and stuffy. Cardboard and carpet remnants lay stacked on the floor, congealed and rotting. Their feet squished as they walked to the back of the container. A dangling curtain marked a doorway cut in the steel. A faint glow emanated from the space on the other side.

Barma shoved the curtain back and stepped through. "Watch the edges. It's sharp."

A second container lay on the opposite side. Bare metal floors and no rust. A single bulb dangled from a wire in the center of the space. A table sat beneath it. And sprawled around the table next to knocked-over chairs lay three bodies.

Miles let out a sharp exhale. "You brought me here for this?"

"Call it what you will. I want a second opinion. And don't put your foot in anything important."

"I know the drill."

Miles crouched and surveyed the scene. Three firearms lay scattered nearby, two burners and a sawed-off shotgun so short it might as well be a pistol. One burner was chrome, a model with four to six shots, personal defense, and not much use otherwise. The second burner was something law enforcement might carry, capable of augmentation uplink, a twelve-shot battery, and high power for a laser pistol. But the battery light was winking red. The shooter had emptied it.

All the weapons were close enough to have been dropped by the three victims. There were personal devices on the floor as well, along with blood from one of the fallen.

"Checked for vitals?" Miles asked. "I assume you did, since there's no ambulance here."

"They're all gone."

Miles shifted closer and shined his own flashlight. All three men were well dressed, relatively neat, groomed, and clean, at least until the event which marked their demise.

The first body, the closest, was a middle-aged white male, patterned silk charcoal suit, a wide necktie with mauve and silver horizontal stripes, and a matching pocket square. Buffed fingernails and cleanly shaven. He had been struck by the shotgun in the chest.

The second man lay on his side, his face partially concealed. Brown skin, older, thin, balding, with long white sideburns. His slender, almost skeletal, fingers still touched the chrome pocket burner. He wore rings on his hands, gold, and most were studded with gems. Tidy laser holes marked his left arm, throat, and cheek.

Miles had to maneuver to examine the third man. The largest of the three, he had fallen backward with his arms out. His yellow coat lay open, revealing his ample stomach and a bright starched white shirt marked with a tiny burner wound over his heart. His sun-bleached blond hair was thin and gelled and looked like a raised palm fixed to the back of his head. A pair of AR glasses sat askew on his face, but Miles didn't see any visible augmentations that would link with the device.

"All wounds are front-facing," Miles said. "Appears that they shot each other."

"Yup. And?"

"Everyone was seated and getting along well enough. None of them look like they live anywhere near here. The one with the glasses might have been recording what went down. I'd check all their devices. Doubt they were meeting for a card game in this dump. Something shady, no doubt."

The marshal grunted. "No doubt. That's all police 101. I didn't call you out here for that."

"All right. I'll bite. Who are they?"

"You really haven't been around here long." Barma used his light to illuminate the big guy in the yellow coat. "Bing Patton. He's the owner of the Yellow Tigers militia, or at least the closest thing. He's the largest stake holder and president of their board of directors."

The thin man was next. "Shahid Khar. If you know the Seraph underworld, you know him. He has fingers in every pot. Information broker. He knows where all the closets are and put some skeletons in there himself. He has leverage on so many people he could move Seraph a hundred klicks in any direction, if he decided it would make him a profit."

Finally, Barma directed the flashlight to the man in the silk suit. "And that's Xander Trowbridge. Old money. Knew the elder Fishes when Seraph was little more than a big camp next to the old springs. Water baron, owns more land than anyone should, whether illegally or by rule of law. Fancies himself the patron saint of Earth's post-Meridian expansion and figures every man, woman, and child owes him obeisance."

"Rarified crowd. And here they are."

Barma took off his hat and sighed. "Yeah. Right outside city limits on my turf."

"And you called me."

"To say this one is complicated is like saying the platinum rock which got dropped in the desert a couple of hundred years ago shook the ground a little. I'm looking at the richest man in Seraph dead next to one of its biggest criminals, alongside the guy who calls the shots of the largest militia. This is going to cause a few ripples. And right now you're the only one I trust enough to eyeball this thing."

"Why me? You have an office of trained marshals."

"Yeah, the others are out. Plus, there isn't one of them who isn't at least a little tainted."

Miles straightened and ignored the complaints from his popping knees. "It happens. But it's the job and what you have to work with. What about the other agencies?"

"Yellow Tiger and Red District militias. And then there's Sheriff Vaca's office, but she just boomerangs everything that takes actual work over to the militias."

"From what I've seen, the militias handle calls outside the city when asked."

Barma gave him an appraising look. "Learn that from Captain Sin? I heard you two were dating."

"Three evenings out watching my son play what he calls music isn't dating."

"Whatever. My office has a specific mandate. Fugitives, court security, protect the mayor and city officials, and first response to major crimes outside of Seraph, from Devil's Bridge and points west and south out to 250 klicks. This one's a squeaker, but you're right. It's ours. Wishing it otherwise won't make it go away. I'm asking you for help."

"I already have a job."

As if on cue, Miles' device vibrated. A text from Tristan. "Dog keeps whining. ETA on your return?"

Miles swiped closed the notification. "Speaking of which, I need to get back."

"Quit. I can put you on the payroll as a deputized consultant."

"No, thanks. I did the cop thing for more years than I care to admit. The security gig pays the rent."

Barma's jaw tightened and he nodded. Set his hat on his head and started texting. "Calling my forensic team out."

Miles studied the walls. Only a couple of burner holes in the steel. Not many misses. Laser pistols rarely penetrated a body. He walked carefully to the far end of the container where the heavy doors stood closed. Muddy footprints abounded, which he avoided. He pushed a door open. A small cul-de-sac lay at the end of an alley lined with more of the shipping crates. Two vehicles were parked in the dirt, one a polished black sedan and the other a Yellow Tiger desert runner.

"This is where they parked," Miles announced.

Barma didn't look up from his screen. "Saw it when I first arrived and checked for any survivors."

"Then you probably counted two vehicles here. Were any of the victims friends?"

"I'd guess they hated each other. This wasn't a social event."

"Yeah. That means two of them either carpooled, or one vehicle is missing."

Science Fiction by I.O. Adler

<u>The Broken Stars series</u>

A stolen spaceship is Earth's last hope of uncovering the truth of what happened on Mars.

Shadows of Mars

Deimos Station

The Star Reliquary

You may also enjoy these science fiction and fantasy novels published by Lucas Ross Publishing

<u>The Minders' War series</u>

For Deanne and her correctional facility work crew, the night the stars fell ended everything.

Refuge

The Glass Heretic

The Children of Magus

<u>The Goblin Reign series</u>

They razed Spicy's village, kidnapped his sister, and never imagined what one lone goblin would do to get her back!

Goblin

Goblin Apprentice

Goblin Rogue

Goblin War Chief

Goblin Outcast

<u>Fallen Rogues</u>

A city of rogues. A seedy bar. A thief who stole the wrong prize.

The Midnight Monster Club

The Dragon and Rose

The Chapel of the Wyrm

The Isle of the Fallen

Printed in Great Britain
by Amazon

14627132R00088